The Worlds Just Out of Sight

Mark Hersch enjoys a busy summer in his favorite
place: with his grandparents in Lightning Gap.
Then one job brings a shiver of warning.
Will Mark and his Papaw see the danger in time?

Ella finds the perfect vacation spot.
Stunning scenery. Fabulous rooms. Decadent food.
Peace and quiet and reconnection.
And a great car and road just for her.
But Paradise hides more than Ella imagined...

Amy gets to relive a cherished childhood memory.
To remember a night full of wonder.
A trip into the past both sweet and melancholy.
But sometimes the past makes other plans.

Paul's best friend Sadie lived a life worth celebrating.
Now Paul carries on her work without her.
Paul never suspects Sadie left a secret just for him.
A secret that changes his life forever.

Kay's Café specializes in comfort. From the greetings
to the decor, and especially the food.
Kay always knows what everybody needs.
But some folks need comfort in a different way.
Can she bring the taste of love itself back to life?

~

Discover five original new stories and an adventure
through the magic of Appalachia and beyond.

STEPPING OUT OF REALITY

SHORT SPELLS OF APPALACHIAN MAGIC

KARI KILGORE

SPIRAL PUBLISHING, LTD.

CONTENTS

INTRODUCTION

Life is full of changes. Transitions.

Portals, if you will.

Even if we don't recognize them at the time, we all live through events that mark our passage through life. From youth to adulthood, from middle age into our senior years. Gaining knowledge and experience, reaching goals, losing friends and loved ones.

Even the joyful transitions leave us changed, sometimes more than the painful ones do.

When I was writing the original stories for this collection, I didn't have a theme or plan in mind aside from the focus on portals. I was a couple of stories in before I realized they'd all be set in my native Appalachian Mountains of Virginia.

Since my family moved away before I turned four and I've resided here on and off since I was nineteen, frequent visits and moves turned this setting into a real-life portal for me.

I always thought of the mountains and valleys

and forests as home, but I was often the outsider returning. With life here tending to run at a slower pace, it was usually me doing the changing, while the land and much of my family remained the same. Returning home with a solidly Midwestern accent sets me apart as well, no matter how many years I stay put.

That dual perspective as an insider and an outsider is one of my most-treasured storytelling gifts.

It comes in pretty handy for life in general, too.

As often happens when I put a collection together, I'm surprised at how the stories seem to organize themselves. In this case, it was those life events, the portals we all pass through in one way or another.

Mark Hersch stands at the threshold of several changes in *The Perfect Shade of Haint Blue*. Learning to drive, considering college, thinking of where and how he wants to begin his adult life. The close relationship with his grandfather—closer to the end of his own time—provides Mark with a vital guide and guardrail.

In *The Road to Paradise Mountain*, Ella Weaver made many of those choices years ago. She's reached the point of deciding what sort of middle age she wants to pursue. In my own experience and in observing the world around me, that's a prime time for a youthful passion to truly come into its own.

And yes, I do indeed love to drive a great car on a beautiful road! I haven't yet found Paradise Mountain, but I'll keep searching.

The restoration of a beloved landmark from Amy Holbrook's youth brings a chance for reliving the past in *Amy in Wonderland*. That's one of the many wonderful opportunities that can come with maturity. Getting to revisit and finally understand childhood events that brought us joy, or pain, or simply confusion.

Paul Weaver faces one of the more difficult passages in *The Lightning-struck Wood*: celebrating a dear friend's life while feeling sad about their absence. The challenge in a situation like that, especially when the friend made a positive impact on many people's lives, is finding a way to remember and honor them with joy.

One way to try to pay respects and keep a loved one's memory alive is by keeping up their traditions. That might be singing a certain song, putting up special holiday decorations, or supporting their favorite charity.

Certainly here in Appalachia and within many other cultures around the country and around the world, that tradition often involves cooking and sharing meals together. In *A Taste Just Like a Hug*, Kay Walton wants nothing more than to comfort friends of hers in that most personal way.

Of course one of the best things about writing my way through these life transitions rather than living them is I get to add fantasy elements (or to be honest, the storytelling engine in my mind adds them for me). When it comes to portal fantasy, those elements can range from an adjustment to the senses all the way to a magical passageway.

These enhancements always surprise me when they show up, especially when their primary job is to amplify what's already happening in the story.

And I'll admit I wish I'd had a few of these extra abilities available to me in real life a time or two.

I hope you enjoy getting to know these characters and reading these stories as much as I enjoyed writing them. Several of the people (and settings) you'll meet in these pages are parts of series. So if you want to join them, and me, on more adventures, you can find out more at the end of the book.

You can also visit www.KariKilgore.com to learn more about me and find other short stories, along with novellas, novels, and more collections.

For more Appalachian stories, head on over to www.KariKilgore.com/TalesfromAppalachia.

You'll discover more fantasy of many kinds at www.KariKilgore.com/Fantasy.

If you want to keep up with what I'm doing next, get free stories, read exclusive content not available anywhere else, and see adorable pet photos, check out www.ConfidentialAdventureClub.com. Hope to see you there!

And last but certainly not least, thank you for your support of me and my writing. It means the world to me and keeps me coming back to tell the next tale.

KARI KILGORE

AUTHOR OF SECRETS IN THE LAND AND THE EARWORMS

The Perfect Shade of Haint Blue

A VOICES THROUGH TIME STORY

*For everyone who knows to take those strange little
hunches seriously*

THE PERFECT SHADE OF
HAINT BLUE

AFTER THREE YEARS in Las Vegas and the Mojave Desert, July rain on his grandparents' tin roof sounded like heaven to Mark Hersch. The endlessly refreshing scent and the feel of clean humidity on his skin only amplified the effect, once he'd gotten over sweating so much for the first week or so.

He kicked one brown hiking boot against the dark blue painted floor of the porch, sending the long porch swing back into motion. Every time he leaned his head against the high back of the swing, he smiled at the contrast of the narrow boards of the ceiling overhead painted a pale robin's egg blue.

Haint blue, his granny called that paint color, her musical Appalachian accent making the word so much more interesting than his own generic military brat pronunciation of *haunt* could ever be.

Mark had heard folks say using that color on the porch was an old Southern and mountain tradition, meant to keep ghosts so confused and disoriented by an apparent blue sky overhead that they never found their way inside.

He suspected there was more to the tradition than that, but hadn't been able to get online to confirm it just yet. The late Nineties had brought fast and easy internet to Vegas, but the slow, creaky dialup deep in the mountains around Hartstown, Virginia, was another frustrating story.

Lugging a big computer tower and monitor all this way hadn't been anywhere near worth the trouble.

When Mark first arrived for his summer stay in early June, the long metal chains holding up the swing sang out with a distinctive groaning noise every time someone pushed back. One of his first help-around-the-house jobs—following his parents' edict that he make himself useful and welcome rather than being a lazy fifteen-year-old nuisance—had been oiling that chain to quiet the sound.

His grandparents both thanked him and claimed to be happy about the nearly silent motion of the swing now, but Mark was sure he caught a flash of sadness in their eyes.

He kept his quiet regret to himself, and how much he missed that otherworldly groan. He was afraid if he told them he felt like he'd stolen the haint's voice, they'd both agree.

And that would be entirely too depressing for summertime.

Mark knew it was useless, but he once again attempted to tame his ornery mop of strawberry blond hair. His fingers only caught on painful snarls, likely making the whole thing worse.

One of the very few things he liked about the dry

climate in Las Vegas was the way his hair *almost* behaved. It was still wavy, sure, and not likely to be anyone's definition of smooth, any more than he was himself.

In the always-humid mountain air, his hair celebrated its liberation by twisting and snaking itself into a tangled mess at the slightest provocation. A late Thursday morning rainstorm after a sweaty, dusty job apparently called for a lively corkscrew party.

More like a rave, really.

His father offered a gentle suggestion a few years ago when it started to curl that Mark might want to keep it cut short, like his own typically close Air Force trim. Mark had rejected that idea outright, even though he wasn't sure why. Now it was long enough to touch his collar out in Vegas, protecting at least a little of him from the brutal sun without requiring gobs of sunscreen.

On days like this, when it curled high on the nape of his neck instead, he wondered if his dad's haircut might not be a good idea after all.

At what he thought was the sound of an engine over the drumming of rain, Mark sat up and looked out across the rain-soaked lawn—the riotous deep green grass and kaleidoscope of his Granny's flowerbeds still surprising to his desert-adjusted eyes. Beyond that, all he could see was mountains rising up all around, thick with oaks and pines and maples.

Sure enough, his Papaw's burgundy Chevy pickup turned onto the short, graveled driveway.

His grandparents had been headed out shopping when Mark caught a ride for one of his countless odd jobs early that morning. Well, his Papaw called it *going trading* instead, at least when he wanted to sound more mountain and hillbilly than he actually was.

Mark jumped up before his Granny could open the door, leaving the swing to carry its ghosts back and forth in silence, and grabbed one of the umbrellas from an old wooden barrel by the porch door. His old jeans and faded brown and gold Bonanza High School t-shirt could stand the soaking after a few hours helping clean out an ancient barn full of junk.

And the very definition of helping around the house surely had to include keeping his Granny from trudging through wet grass in the rain.

His Papaw unfolded his lanky self from the driver's side, opening a bright yellow umbrella as he stood. Mark's father said Papaw was the source of all the unruly hair in the family, and the strawberry blond color, too. But the senior Mr. Hersch kept his silver locks too short to show any curl.

One thing Mark knew for sure was something clicked between him and his Papaw, something that made sense in a way it never quite had with his parents. He loved his mom and dad and they all got along, but he was as quietly puzzled by them as they were by him.

With Papaw, and most of the time with Granny, Mark had the unusual comfort of not trying to figure out how to be anyone but himself, even when he wasn't quite sure who that would turn out to be.

"What are you doing sitting out here, water bug?" Papaw said with his gravelly voice and big smile. "Can't imagine you already forgot where the key is."

Mark laughed and shook his head as he reached the passenger side of the truck. His Papaw had been calling him water bug for as long as he could remember, apparently inspired by the impossibility of keeping him out of puddles and streams and creeks, even as a toddler.

Mark had gotten a little bit better at keeping himself from getting muddy, but he was still endlessly fascinated with water.

"I remember where it is, mud bug," Mark said. "I was just enjoying the rain. We don't get this much in a year in Vegas."

Mark's Granny stepped out under the open umbrella, beaming up at him. Her lively bright green eyes were the same ones Mark saw in the mirror every day.

She was as compact and economical as Papaw was long and tall, and her shiny brunette hair hardly ever seemed to misbehave. Any stray silver that threatened to gain a foothold was quickly and cheerfully wiped out with the assistance of Miss Clairol.

Standing beside his grandmother, Mark hoped all the talk about growth spurts still to come turned out to be true. He loved his Granny dearly, but he didn't love the idea of ending up only a couple of inches taller than her five-three.

Not that he'd quite gotten there yet.

"Why thank you, Mark," she said, squeezing his arm. "It surely is a pleasure having you around here this summer."

"Be sure to tell Dad that next time he calls. I think he's still convinced I'm slouching around doing nothing but watching TV." He handed her the umbrella, then reached into the truck's cramped back seat before she could. Every square inch was stuffed full of paper and plastic bags from more than one store in town. "I'll get these, go on ahead inside."

She shook her head, still smiling, but she took the umbrella's curved black handle while Mark gathered up two bags full of groceries, still cold from their recent home in the freezer case.

"You're working yourself half to death is what you're doing," she said. "You got to slow down and enjoy at least a little bit of your summer is what I say. Awful good time to meet other kids your age, maybe even a nice girl or two."

Mark did his best to pretend he couldn't feel his cheeks turning red. He hoped that potential growth and eventually learning how to wrangle the disorderly mess on top of his head would open up his dating prospects.

Talking to his Granny or pretty much anyone else about his lack of female companionship wasn't his favorite way to pass the time.

"It might be a perfect time for meeting girls," he said, "but then I'd be heading back out west in a few weeks. It's not exactly nice to leave a trail of broken hearts behind me."

Laughing like a merry songbird and ignoring Mark's protests that he wouldn't melt, she walked beside him along the big slabs of limestone that made up the walkway, now gleaming and dark gray.

"Anyway, I'm enjoying my summer just fine, Granny. Learning a lot, saving up for college, spending time with you two. That reminds me, one of the other guys cleaning out that barn today mentioned the Hartsocks needing some help with their basement today and tomorrow. Something about switching from a coal furnace to gas."

Papaw spoke up sharp from right behind them, carrying his own bags of groceries.

"That's Jessie and Wanda Hartsock? Out on Mulberry Road?"

Mark stepped up onto the porch and to the side to get out of their way. He hardly ever heard that tone in his grandfather's voice unless a bunch of rowdy kids—or the rowdy adults who came with them—started causing trouble during a big family gathering.

"I think so. He might have said Mulberry Road. I won't ask if you know the Hartsocks since you know everybody in Boun County."

Granny rolled her eyes as she dug into her big blue leather purse for her set of keys. Mark suspected he was the only one who was willing to go back out into the rain and get the set hidden under a specific rock in the second flower bed to the right.

"I know the Hartsocks, sure," Papaw said, his brow wrinkling. "Good folks, not a thing in the world wrong with you helping them out. I heard Jessie talking about that new furnace, how it will be so much easier on him than shoveling coal. But I'm real sorry to admit I don't much like the idea of you going out there on your own."

Mark frowned, but a quick little thrill of excitement shot through his belly.

He really did mean to earn some extra money and spend time with his grandparents. The change of pace and scenery was already doing him a world of good, especially since he was seriously considering coming right back to Virginia for college in a couple of years.

But he wouldn't mind a bit of mystery and adventure to spice things up while he was here.

"Did something strange happen there, Papaw? At the Hartsock place?"

"Well no, I can't exactly say that. It's just... I got an uneasy twinge about you going there is all. Not by yourself for sure."

Now he had every bit of Mark's attention. His father and everyone else in the family often talked about Papaw's twinges, and hunches, and notions, and even dreams. No one ever made much of a fuss about it that Mark could tell.

But they never mentioned thinking those twinges were something it was better to ignore, either.

Granny snorted as she finally found her keys.

"I get the feeling you're going to have to do better than that, Walt. This particular grandson is an awful lot like you. Stores up every little thing in his mind, and already thought up about a thousand questions. When did they need you over there, Mark?"

Mark shrugged. "Sounded to me like they were getting started on some of it this afternoon. Clearing out room for the new furnace. I told them I'd talk to you, then call if I couldn't make it."

"There you go," Granny said, nodding once as she opened the door. "Sounds to me like you two might want to take a little trip out to Mulberry Road after lunch. Good time for Mark to practice driving the truck anyway. We can't hardly send him back out West until he's better with the stick shift."

Papaw blew air out his lips and shook his head, but he was smiling. Mark couldn't resist grinning in return.

"What that sounds to *me* like is your Granny

wants some time to herself after putting up with me on her big shopping trip," Papaw said. "I'll tell you right now that is one of the main secrets of a good marriage, Mark. Both of you knowing when to get out for a little while. If you don't mind me going along, I wouldn't mind a chat with Jessie. And I suppose you need more practice driving in the mountains."

"I don't mind one bit, Papaw. Hope your truck's transmission is up for it."

~

AN HOUR AND A HALF LATER, Mark was fairly sure he wasn't doing the Chevy's gears and clutch too much damage. He'd improved over the last few weeks until he only heard that telltale grind a couple of times on the drive along Hartsfield's curving mountain back roads.

The truck itself was more disorienting after learning in the compact car his father drove to the Air Force base and back and his mother's good-sized sedan they all rode in together. Both automatic, neither one putting him so strangely *high* above the ground.

And while he found his Papaw's good-natured presence and occasional advice reassuring, Mark felt like he sat on the other side of a big living room rather than in the same vehicle. A living room scented with his Papaw's Old Spice and spearmint gum, and his Granny's coffee. One where his chair had to be scooted forward quite a bit so his feet could reach the pedals.

So far so good keeping to his side of the narrow

roads, full of blind curves and most of them without lines down the middle to help. Attempting to steer the wide truck without taking up way more than his fair share of the lane kept him gripping the huge steering wheel harder than he should. The constant refrain from his mother, father, and now his grandfather to try and relax instead of knotting up into a tense ball of worry seemed a thousand miles from possible.

Thankfully the rain had finally let up before they headed out. Worrying about hitting a big puddle and hydroplaning was more than enough to pay attention to.

Driving around Vegas on dry suburban and city streets hardly prepared him for this.

His parents and grandparents and older kids kept saying he'd be driving without having to think about every little thing before he knew it, but he had his doubts.

And yet he loved every single second.

As he came out of a long, steep curve and saw a straight stretch long enough to take a deep breath, his Papaw reminded him of another of his parents' driving suggestions.

Watch the road, always, and remember that's your most important job. But conversation sure can make the time go by.

"Okay, the way gets a little bit easier from here on out, Mark. You're doing real good."

"Starting to get the hang of it at least. You never did tell me what made you worry about me going to the Hartsocks' house. What happened there? Or what do you *think* could happen?"

Papaw let out his rough-edged laugh, more vocal

evidence of what he called a leftover from his hard-living youth. Before he got married and civilized.

"Your Granny was right about you, water bug. You just keep right on paying close attention and asking your questions, hear? That will do you good for the rest of your life." He paused and took his own deep breath. "Nothing strange ever did happen out at the Hartsock place, not to me or anyone I heard tell of. More than their share of trouble, sure, but ordinary. Out here in the world, anyway."

Mark shifted his tense shoulders down and back, turning the words over in his mind.

Almost all of his visits here had been crowded and full. With his swarm of cousins, aunts, and uncles, or at least his parents. That was one reason this time was so precious

He couldn't recall ever getting a chance to ask his Papaw about this without everyone else chiming in.

"You mean it was a story you heard from someone else? Like a tall tale? Or more like one of your hunches?"

"A tall tale means someone else is telling it, or at least heard it passed around. This one came right from me, and you're the first to hear it. I can't recall it too clearly, but I had a dream about that house not long ago. It had pretty much slipped my mind until I heard you say their name."

"Something bad happened to *me* in your dream?"

After a few seconds of silence, Mark risked a quick glance to his right. Papaw didn't look overly scared or worried, but the way he pressed his lips into a thin line meant he was thinking something over.

"I can't quite bring it to mind as clear as all that.

Only that I don't feel like you should be out there alone. Or without me along, I should say. Turn right once you get past this curve and be sure to hit your blinker."

Mark navigated the sharp left curve, then put the turn signal on when he spotted a gravel road ahead.

"But not so bad that you don't think I should be there at all," he said. "Or else you wouldn't have agreed to come out here with me."

"I'd say that's pretty much the way it is. The thought of you going there scared me enough to get my attention, but not enough to stop you. I learned over the years of dealing with these bad feelings I get that I'm gonna do better if I heed them. Even if that means your Granny or you or anyone else looks at me funny. It was when I tried to fight them that I got myself into trouble. People around me, too."

The truck left the pavement with more of a jolt than Mark expected. A second after his teeth clacked together, he realized the puddle right there must be deeper than he thought. He managed to get the truck downshifted in that tiny gap between the engine starting to chug and stalling out.

"Sorry about that. Just tell me if you think there's anything I should be careful of, okay? Or anybody."

"Don't you worry, this big old truck can handle a lot worse than that. I don't reckon you'll have trouble with anybody. Jessie and Wanda are both good folks. Doing a real good job getting the house fixed up after he inherited it in such a terrible shape. That was a hard thing all the way around. If it had been Jessie's father or grandfather asking you to help out, I would have flat told you no, mostly grown at fifteen years old or not."

"I know I probably shouldn't ask, but I'm going to be nosy anyway. What was going on with his family before now?"

"Watch for this road to split not far along, you'll want to keep to the left. I don't guess there's any harm in telling you, since you're not the kind to run out and gossip. Jessie's people were forever getting into trouble, almost always because of their own doings. Never seemed to meet a crooked deal or plan they didn't like. They might have had you helping move things that was stolen, or illegal to begin with."

"Sounds like some of the old organized crime stuff I've heard about out in Vegas. Heard rumors they operated here in the mountains, too, during Prohibition. I won't mention anything about the Hartsocks."

He slowed again, following the bumpy gravel road to the left. A good-sized creek alongside ran hard enough to roar even with the windows rolled up.

"According to what might have been nothing more than your tall tales, pretty much everything ran through here during those dry years. Anything folks could drink or make a buck on, for sure. You'll see the driveway up on the right here in a minute. Be sure you downshift before you start up. It's a good bit steeper than it looks."

Mark blinked and barely managed not to gasp when he caught sight of the gray slash cutting through the trees and underbrush at what looked like an impossible angle, worse than any staircase he'd seen.

If that road was *steeper* than it looked, he was never going to make it.

"Maybe you should take over," he said, already easing back on the gas. "Rolling us over the side of the mountain wasn't on my schedule for the day."

"No, you'll do just fine, Mark. It's just a road you got to pay attention to like any other. Here, go on ahead and drop the transmission down to four, then three, so you won't be worrying about that. Stay on the inside away from that drop off on this first part and you won't have any trouble."

Mark doubted anyone else would be on a gravel road this isolated, but several loud voices inside his head insisted he check both ways before he did anything else. He pushed the clutch down with his left foot, then moved the gearshift to fourth gear. The engine wound up a little as it slowed, pushing him forward against the seatbelt. One more shift to third, and he ignored his knotted shoulder and back muscles and carefully guided the truck onto the insane-looking road.

"What if I stall it out? I don't think I can get us going again."

"Slow and steady, that's all. If you get into real trouble, you know I'll help you fix it."

Those words, and something about the confident way Papaw said them, let a good bit of the tension drain away.

Thankfully the curves weren't as sharp as Mark feared, and the Chevy really did feel like it could climb straight up a wall if he took the right approach. After only a few minutes passing through trees growing up close to the road with branches low overhead, he spotted a clearing opening up ahead.

Then a house that looked like it was built right into the side of the mountain.

The first part—made out of a row of cinderblocks dark gray with the rain—was too short, with a solid wooden door Mark thought even he would have to duck to walk through. That had to be the basement, and home of the old coal furnace. A graveled path in front already had a pile of what looked like old bits of machinery.

A second level with regular white siding that looked brand new sat above and behind that, with more cinderblocks painted brown making a diagonal stairway to the tiny landing and front door. Still another level sat farther back, this one with only windows.

In front of the basement and in a steep slope on the left side of the house, a narrow band of grass separated the yard from the trees. The driveway spread out to the right into several little terraces that were mostly flat, making room for two other pickup trucks.

Mark smiled to himself when he spotted a side door with a little overhang that was freshly painted haint blue. And he smiled even bigger when he realized one of those clever gravel terraces was big enough for him to park in with no trouble at all.

He held in the brake and clutch, turned the engine off, and pushed the parking brake pedal with his left foot to make sure his nightmare scenario of helplessly watching the truck roll away didn't come true.

When he finally pulled the keys out of the ignition, he let out a big enough breath to fog up his half of the massive windshield.

He turned to give his Papaw the keys, and saw a huge, proud grin.

"Knew you'd do fine, water bug. Just think, you never have to do that for the first time again. Hang onto the keys if you might want to drive us back home."

Mark laughed and shook his head as he dropped the keys into Papaw's big, rawboned hand.

"I might want to drive us home once I get over driving us up here," he said as they got out. "Last thing I want to do is lose them before we ever get to that point."

The sky was still overcast like it had been for a few days, and the air was much cooler than when they'd started out so much farther down. A breeze scented with the rich, green smell of the nearby forest raised goosebumps along Mark's arms. He'd need the long-sleeved shirt they'd brought if the basement was even colder.

Despite the gloom and chill, the trees echoed with birdsong.

A man dressed in dingy coveralls stepped out of the basement door, raising his chin in a typical guy reverse-nod. He wore a green baseball cap that covered his hair, and his face was too long and thin to guess his age, other than a generic over-thirty.

"Hey there, Walt," he said. "Bring us someone else to help clear out this mess?"

"Sure did, Jessie. This here's my grandson Mark. Figured I'd better come along to keep everyone in line."

Jessie stepped forward to shake hands, enveloping Mark's in his rough, warm grip.

"Good to meet you, young man. Got a grandson about the same age as you, but he already sprouted up to near six foot tall. Can't hardly keep him fed these days. Looks like you're about to do the same thing. Need anything to eat or drink before we get started?"

"No thank you, Mr. Hartsock. It's a big job, but they keep me pretty well fed and watered."

Both men laughed, and Mr. Hartsock clapped Mark on the shoulder.

"Sounds like we'll get along just fine as long as you call me Jessie. Come on inside and see what kind of mess you're about to get into."

When Jessie ducked back into the basement, Mark turned back to his Papaw, eyebrows raised.

He wanted to help, and he'd be happy to have the money and the experience. But if Papaw said one of those twinges rose up too strong, Mark would turn right back around and get both of them out of there.

Papaw hesitated for a second, then nodded once.

"Feels all right for now. Both of us can keep a watch out and speak up if that changes. Okay?"

"Okay. I'll start by saying watch out and don't bump your head on the door, mud bug."

The basement was bigger than it looked from the outside, but no one would call it spacious. The walls were cut out of what looked like limestone, the same bedrock Mark knew made up a lot of the mountains from his study of geology. Pretty much the only thing that fascinated him almost as much as water.

The huge, age-darkened beams of the house itself a few feet overhead held a handful of bare lightbulbs, but no way upstairs besides cobweb-covered duct-work like an upside down spider reaching into all the corners.

Even in the bright light, he couldn't tell if the floor was dirt or just dirty. From the looks of the ancient, soot-crusted coal furnace in the middle of the room, it could be either one. Stacks of what looked like broken furniture and appliances, or maybe tools for working in the yard, ran along the walls. One corner still held a coal pile nearly as high as his waist.

The organic, faintly sulfuric aroma of the burned coal itself hung heavy in the air, along with an oddly damp smell Mark couldn't quite place, and that didn't make sense in the dry basement.

A smell that sent a shiver through him that had nothing to do with the cold air inside.

Jessie stood beside the furnace, hands on his hips.

"I know there's a bunch to do, and I planned to get most of it done myself. But yesterday I got a call that the installer can make it out tomorrow. A week *early*, if you can believe that. Had someone else cancel. I'm not afraid to admit I just want to get it all over and done with."

He shrugged and grabbed a pair of brown leather work gloves and handed them to Mark.

"Ain't no telling what all my people tried to hide away down here, so you best protect your hands. All this dust and stink, we should probably be wearing some kind of masks. Anyway, a couple of other boys are going to try and stop by later if this gets to be too much."

"Even if we can't get it all loaded into the trucks," Mark said, "the installers should have plenty of room to work here in a couple of hours. Let's see how much we can get done."

A bunch of heavy loads later—including a puzzling collection of lawnmower handles with no sign of the lawnmowers—Mark had no need of the long-sleeved shirt still waiting in his Papaw's truck.

Even if he had wished for it a few times when disturbed spiders tried to escape up his arms. Thankfully not a one that had the shiny body and red hourglass of the black widows he'd learned to watch out for in Las Vegas.

He didn't miss having to watch out for scorpions, either.

He and Jessie had carried out a set of rusty bedsprings, a badly rusted hand-crank washer, and several paint cans so old they flaked and crumbled to the touch. Papaw had insisted on doing his part, especially once Mark uncovered a wheelbarrow that looked more or less sturdy.

They still had enough room to get by out on the little walkway in front of the basement, but only just.

"Reckon we're about down to carrying most of this junk out to the trucks once those other boys get here." Jessie stretched with his hands pressed into the small of his back. "You been working like a champ, Mark, so I'll let you pick. Want to start on that, or start loading up that coal pile into the wheelbarrow?"

Mark pulled off one glove to wipe sweat from his forehead, making sure not to get into what had to be the even worse tangle of his hair. He'd worked enough over the summer to know he'd be tired tonight, but not too bad. He expected to put away the huge dinner Granny would put in front of him, take a long, hot shower, then sleep like a log all night long.

Jessie was dragging, though, and Mark wasn't about to let his Papaw shovel coal.

"I'll start on the coal if you can point me toward a shovel. Might take me a while, but that's just as well.

I wouldn't want the others to show up and not have anything left to do."

Papaw and Jessie laughed and shook their heads.

"I sure would like to have some of your energy," Jessie said. "There's an old shovel against the wall behind the furnace, but it might turn to splinters in your hand soon as you pick it up. I managed to break the good one at the end of last winter and only got around to getting a new one yesterday. Let me run out to the truck and grab it. That and some home-made lemonade in a jug that Wanda left for us up in the kitchen."

"I'll fetch the shovel," Papaw said. "Since I sure would like some of that lemonade. You okay, Mark?"

Mark pulled his glove back on and waved both hands toward the door.

"I'm good, Papaw. I'll yell if I find something awful buried down in all that coal."

Papaw raised one eyebrow, but only for a second.

"I'll be right back, then."

Mark stretched with his hands overhead, glancing around at the newly empty room. As he walked toward the massive iron bulk of the furnace, he wondered if Jessie—and more importantly his Papaw—would let him help the installers tomorrow.

If nothing else, he wanted to see how they got the heavy thing out of there.

With a blowtorch, maybe?

Or would they just bring in some kind of big saw instead?

He stepped around beside the furnace.

One of the few places that had been empty when they walked in.

One arm out to grab the shovel, most of his mind on the next day.

Instead of the thud of solid ground, he heard a hollow thump.

And his feet broke through into nothing at all.

Mark tried to shout, but a shock of freezing cold stole all of his breath.

Stinking water splashed above his head as he plunged under.

Even as he commanded himself not to panic, his heart raced and he had to force himself not to try to gulp in air.

But his soaking wet jeans and boots threatened to keep him sinking.

His flailing hand hit something and he grabbed on tight.

An icy horizontal bar that felt like metal.

Mark grabbed it with both hands and shoved himself upward.

His knuckles scraped painfully across rock, then smashed into something harder.

Another bar!

He hauled himself higher and almost shouted when he realized it had to be a ladder.

One more rung, and his head finally broke through into a floating jumble of broken wood and strips of what looked like black fabric.

Mark screamed before he even pulled himself out of the water.

"Papaw!"

He was in a ragged hole not much wider than his own two arms, and amazed to see he was only a few feet below the basement floor. Only two rungs were visible above the water's yellowish-brown surface.

It reeked of sulfur, as if he'd fallen straight through into hell.

He'd barely gotten his head above the weird jagged edge when his Papaw bellowed from behind him.

"Mark! Hang on!"

A big, warm hand grasped Mark's wrist and nearly dragged him out onto the basement floor. Mark didn't realize he'd gotten at least a mouthful of the water until he coughed and hacked it back up.

"Get all that poison out, Mark, come on now."

Papaw helped him sit up and pounded a little bit too hard on his back.

"I'm okay," he choked out between coughs. "About half frozen, but okay."

"What happened?" Jessie yelled from behind them both. "Mark? Walt?"

Papaw switched from pounding to a hug almost as hard, but a whole heck of a lot more comforting.

"He broke through into a pit or something, filled full of foul rotten water."

Mark sat back and looked around his Papaw's shoulder, where Jessie stood with fists clenched and mouth hanging open. A big glass jug with lemons all over it sat at his feet.

Papaw grabbed Mark's shoulders and leaned close, looking into his eyes. His own were wide and terrified.

"I'm so sorry, Mark. I never should have left you in here alone. I knew better, and I *told* you so, but I did it anyway like a damn fool."

Mark shook his head and wiped stinging water away from his eyes with shaking hands. His heart still pounded and his lungs weren't exactly happy with him, but the panic was starting to loosen its grip.

"Listen to me, Papaw, I'm okay. You *did* tell me. You were right, and I know to listen to you about things like this. I knew better, too. I should have walked right back outside with you."

Jessie squatted beside them, both knees going off like shotguns.

"Oh my god... I had no idea that was there. What is it, a damn *tunnel*? I'll run right back upstairs and get you a big bunch of towels, Mark, or maybe we should get you into the shower."

Mark managed to laugh with only a little bit of a cough at the end.

Now that he was back out of that horrible freezing darkness, even if it was into a dusty, spider-filled basement, he already felt a thousand times better.

This was going to make a *fantastic* story once he got back out to Vegas.

"I think your wife would kill me if I walked through your house like this, don't you? If you've got a hose outside, I'll let you two spray me down, and dry off with a couple of your oldest towels. What I want most of all is a good long drink of that lemonade."

BY THE TIME Jessie made it back down with towels and a bundle of clothes his grandson had outgrown, Mark had already stripped down to his underwear. He'd managed to hose himself off from head to toe with water that actually felt warm compared to what was under the basement floor.

His Papaw ducked back out of the basement about the time Mark started spraying the soggy mess of his clothes piled up on the gravels.

"Whoever built that tunnel did the job right," Papaw said with a ghost of a smile. He was still too pale and a little shaky, but he didn't look nearly as bad as a few minutes ago. "Laid down a layer of tarpaper under the wood, then shoveled dirt over top of that. No telling when anyone would have found it with the tarpaper keeping the smell of that water down."

Mark scrubbed his hair, trying not to think how much trouble it was going to be to drag a comb through later.

"You mean before I managed to step right through. What do you think it was for, Jessie?"

Jessie shook his head and handed Mark a clean pair of jeans.

"Lord only knows with that bunch, and that's the honest truth. From what I heard, they ran anything and everything, long as they weren't supposed to. It's rained so much this spring and summer that it might not have been flooded like that before. I was hardly ever down there except shoving coal in wintertime. I wouldn't be surprised if they hid people down there half the time instead of some kind of treasure."

"I expect someone can get that water pumped out," Papaw said. "One of the mining outfits, or maybe someone out at one of the colleges. Pretty sure they teach geology and such out in Blacksburg at Virginia Tech."

Mark gladly accepted a Hartsfield high school t-shirt, faded to a perfect shade of haint blue.

Of course if he'd gotten a big enough lungful of that polluted water, or hit his head on the ladder instead of grabbing hold of it, he might have become the haint himself.

"I hope this doesn't cause you trouble tomorrow," he said. "With the new furnace, I mean."

Jessie guffawed until he wiped tears from his eyes.

"That's the last thing that would ever cross my mind after what happened, Mark. The furnace will get done when it gets done. Most important thing is you being safe and sound."

Papaw handed Mark his long-sleeved shirt, blinking back his own tears.

"You sure are right about that, Jessie," Papaw said. "Not one thing in the world matters more."

His Papaw's words drove away the last of Mark's chill better than anything else ever could.

KARI KILGORE

AUTHOR OF ODDS AND ENDINGS AND INTENTIONS

The Road to Paradise Mountain

*For women everywhere
who understand that sometimes*

it's all about the drive

Chapter 1

THE ROAD to Paradise Mountain Resort more than lived up to its promise as far as Ella Weaver was concerned. The location in the remote and secluded mountains in the far western tip of Virginia was enough to earn the name.

Endless acres of forested mountains, bathed in the stunning pinks, yellows, and purples of trees waking up for springtime. Ella had to work to convince herself she wasn't looking at rolling ocean waves reflecting back a brilliant sunrise.

The main lodge could have been the stand-in for a grand lodge in a national park even though the resort was private. Set in an open meadow with mountains all around, three stories made of huge, rough-cut gray stone, with plenty of windows to take in stunning views in every direction.

All around the lodge, broad swaths of daffodils and tulips continued the colors from the trees, while a creek brimming with snowmelt provided a musical counterpoint to the songs of robins and brilliant red cardinals greeting the very early morning.

From the narrow balcony of their third-floor suite, Ella could just see the edge of the tennis court where she and her husband Jacob had spent a few laughing, profoundly unskilled hours the day before. Straight ahead, across all those flowers and not-quite-green-yet grass, the hiking trail they'd explored the day before headed for miles into the canopy of trees.

With all that sudden activity after a long winter, the balcony's cool tile felt wonderful on her bare feet.

The indoor pool and hot springs spa waited out of sight on the other side of the lodge, but neither one could compete with the intimacy of the big soaking tub in their suite's bathroom.

Even the coffee from the steaming mug currently warming her hands was rich and decadent, almost as much as the thick terrycloth robe she'd wrapped up in after her shower. Both the robe and the mug were the resort's signature slatey blue that perfectly matched the mountains farthest in the distance. If the past few days were any indication, as soon as Jacob finally woke, they'd head down to the first-floor dining room for a breakfast wonderful enough to savor, and big enough to keep them going for hours.

The resort kept their own cows and hens and got as much as they possibly could from local farmers to help supply vacation fuel for guests lucky enough to book rooms.

Ella had reserved this week-long getaway nearly a year ago.

A soft, wood smoke-scented breeze pushed the robe around her knees and lifted her short brown hair. Warmer than the day before, and with the promise of a pleasant bit of humidity in the air. Only enough fluffy clouds in the clear sky to emphasize the intense blue to come.

Quite a change of pace from still-dreary Michigan this time of year.

Ella and Jacob started the tradition of these spring trips when they were first married almost twenty-five years ago. Partly as a way to escape the drudgery of the long Midwestern winter. Partly in a starry-eyed effort to recapture the relaxation and joy of their European honeymoon.

Taking turns making the big destination decision seemed like the only fair way to handle it.

Jacob often picked beachy places, where the recreational activities were limited to swimming, sunbathing, and enjoying far more exotic food and drink than the resort's fresh eggs, tangy yogurt, perfectly spicy sausage, and unbelievably light and delicious biscuits with plenty of apple butter.

Ella, on the other hand, too often found herself feeling...*restricted* on that kind of vacation. Stuck in one spot, and more antsy than relaxed. She often escaped on boat tours or walking tours. Anything to get moving and explore.

That was another way the Road to Paradise Mountain Resort was her perfect choice.

The *road* part of the name not only meant the long, twisting, gorgeous drive to the lodge itself.

The vast acreage was also home to a fabulous network of roads meant for the best kind of driving.

Beautiful. Challenging. And *fast*.

Created from the old logging paths often blasted right into the mountains, as expertly paved as the best Autobahn in Germany. Experiencing that automotive adrenaline rush for herself in a high-horse-power car happened to be Ella's favorite non-Jacob memory from their honeymoon. She'd never quite hit that high behind the wheel since.

Not yet, anyway. But she hadn't given up looking for it.

And so going for a long drive was exactly what Ella planned to do today.

A long, groaning yawn let her know Jacob was up and about a few seconds before he slipped his arms around her waist.

"That coffee smells almost as good as you do," he whispered close to her ear, sending goosebumps chasing down her arms and legs.

"There's plenty left for you, lazybones. Got all your Extra-Chill Jacob Day plans set up?"

He kissed her cheek and stepped forward to join her at the balcony rail. His curly red bed-head hair stood up sweet and adorable.

"Sure do. After we stuff ourselves silly down-stairs, I'll have a nice, long shower. Then I have a date with a book or two in the library in front of the fire. A refreshing swim after lunch, then a massage so I'll be all nice and pretty for you for dinner. You and your lead foot ready to go?"

Ella grinned and bumped shoulders with him, thankful a thousand times over that even though he didn't share her passion for driving, he understood it. Not only did he happily let her drive on road trips and these vacations, he also encouraged her to take advantage of prime opportunities like this.

"*So* ready to go. They should have my dream car for the day warmed up and waiting for me by the time I get down there. Not all that much of a lead foot day today, more a scenic joyride. Only one car on each track, too, so I'll have all that gorgeous blacktop and outrageous mountain scenery to myself."

"And you'll scope out where you're going to take me tomorrow. What kind of road beast did you get today?"

Ella shook her head, still amazed at her good fortune.

"Only my favorite car in the whole world. Would you believe they have a freaking *Morgan*? Right-place steering wheel and everything."

Jacob blinked and raised his eyebrows, then smiled and put his arm around her shoulders.

"Wow. If my memory of your first time driving one is right, you're going to be in a fantastic mood when you get back. And that makes me the luckiest guy in the whole world."

Chapter 2

THE RESORT'S vast garage looked like a big, traditional horse barn at first glance.

Made of the same gray stones as the lodge and built long and low, it featured a row of broad wooden doors painted the resort's signature slate blue rather than windows. But Ella had never seen a horse barn on any of their trips that opened onto a wide surface of smooth, gleaming black asphalt.

The big difference kicked in with a glimpse at the handful of doors that stood open.

Rather than wooden stalls and stacks of hay, each bay featured more of that same perfect asphalt. And rows of shiny red metal shelves and drawers took the place of combs and saddles around the edges, with fresh tires and tools and books stacked up wherever they fit.

Everything you'd need to maintain a beast made of horse*power* rather than the original horses.

Outside one of those open doors sat the object of

Ella's desire—for the day and for all the decades since she'd first seen one in an old library book.

The deep green Morgan sat sturdy and low, reflecting its storied racing pedigree. The curves of the long front and shorter back fenders looked more like the crouch of a powerful big cat than any kind of car. The hood itself took up more than half the length, with a black leather strap across the top the perfect touch.

The morning's bright sunshine glinted off the smooth, silvery arc of the grille—the first thing that caught her attention that fateful day. A straight grill, even with the proper chrome lines, never looked right to her eye again.

Ella's mind supplied the proper name for the Morgan's paint color without her prompting, repeating words she'd memorized in her love-struck daze at twelve years old.

Connaught Green.

The exact right color.

The Morgan's ragtop was nowhere in sight, leaving the cockpit open to the crisp air.

Exactly as it should be.

She set down her special day bag from the resort—full of water, snacks, with her sunglasses and wallet and smartphone inside. She stepped forward, meaning to reach in and touch the steering wheel, wrapped in the same rich brown leather as the low-slung seats, when a man with a faint English accent spoke from behind her.

"What do you think?"

Ella turned to see a sportscar mechanic out of her personal version of central casting. A little taller than her, built as sturdy as the Morgan, with steel-gray hair under a rounded houndstooth cap. He wore jeans and slate blue jacket with *Road to Paradise Mountain* embroidered over a stylized logo of a stripe of black pavement climbing a jagged peak.

His clothes and hands were all neat and clean, but she had no doubt he would sling himself under any of the cars sheltering in the barn and get to work. She would do the same given half a chance.

"She's a beauty," Ella said in a breathy voice that sounded a bit too much like that girl sitting cross-legged in the middle of the library shelves all those years ago. She did better on the second try. "Sorry, I'm Ella Weaver, and I certainly hope this is my car for the day."

He laughed, the joyful sound of it bringing a smile to Ella's face.

"Wonderful to meet you, Ella. Jack Hughes. No need to apologize for your enthusiasm. It only means you've come to the right place. This is very much your car for the day, and for the rest of your stay if you like."

Ella didn't bother trying to tone down her grin. If she couldn't act like that obsessed kid here of all places—where she'd come to act out those youthful fantasies in her late forties—she'd be missing the point of the whole vacation.

"I would *love* that. My husband Jacob will have to see this car to believe it."

Jack dropped an old-fashioned metal key into her hand, attached to a black leather fob. The familiar Morgan logo--wide-spread wings with a wheel in the middle—was deeply embossed into the leather.

She would have sworn she felt a tingle of magic when she closed her fingers over it.

The shivery anticipation the wide open road and a car ready and eager to go.

"Your husband isn't joining you for your joyride today?" he said over his shoulder as he stepped back into the garage.

Ella let out a laugh of her own, delighted at Jack using the same way she'd described her day to Jacob earlier.

Joyride.

"This is our solo mid-vacation break, where we each get to do our own thing without worrying about the other being antsy. He's more of an appreciative passenger than a driver. To tell you the truth, taking a day to myself for a drive is one of my favorite things, vacation or not."

"That's a lovely tradition. I'll look forward to meeting Jacob tomorrow, then." Jack handed her a small stack of folded, thick paper. "I've put together a packet for you. A map of your course today, just in case you prefer it to the GPS unit. Information about scenic stops along the way, assuming you want to stop. You'll be sharing the way until you reach course number eight. Then you'll truly have the day to yourself with nearly thirty miles ahead of you to explore as you will."

Ella turned back toward the gorgeous car, waiting patiently for her to get in and *go*.

After a careful look at the swirl-patterned wood of the dashboard, with its iconic collection of rounded dials and gauges, she finally spotted the rectangular black screen. Instead of conspicuous and jarring right in the middle, it was tucked into an empty space to the right of the steering wheel beside the low curve of the door.

"I had to hunt for the GPS," she said. "You have it well-hidden."

Jack nodded, pride clear in the way his eyes lit up.

"It would surely be a shame to ruin the lines of such a classic with a great blot of technology. I can remove it if you like."

"No, it's fine," Ella said. "I adore the maps for this kind of occasion. But I'm used to driving with gadgets."

Jack gave a wistful sigh.

"Aren't we all these days? Too many couldn't read a map properly if they tried. Now, your reservation says you're comfortable with manual shift and right-place steering, and that you're experienced in high-speed driving. You've visited a closed driving track before, I take it?"

"Whenever I get the chance without having to pay the five or six figure initiation fee most of them want. A couple of training schools too. This one is different, though, and not just because we can actually fit it into our travel budget. I've never seen one with so many long courses. I can't imagine I'd get tired of Paradise Mountain in a month, much less a week."

Jack waved to what looked like another mechanic walking toward one of the big doors, this time a young woman wearing more typical coveralls. He turned back to Ella with a sparkle in his eyes.

"We were quite fortunate to find this special property when we did, and with so much potential for our peculiar sport. I get the feeling you'll find all the excitement you're looking for. Just remember to drive in the American style until you're on your own private motorway."

At those words, Ella was finished with conversation, even with a pleasant man with a charming accent.

After all, how often did her own private motorway await?

"Not too high-speed today, I think. I'll be busy trying to work out whether the car or the scenery is more beautiful. And more exciting."

Jack laughed again and shook his head.

"You must be sure to tell me what you decide. Pardon me for saying so, but you sound like my dear auntie. She loved driving like no one I've ever seen. I hope you enjoy your day as much as she would have."

He swept off his cap and gestured toward where the broad pavement narrowed into a proper road before it curved into the tree line and out of sight. A big sign—in the resort's special blue rather than typical highway blue or green—declared:

All Driving Courses This Way

By Reservation Only.

Ella grabbed her day bag and dropped it into the passenger seat, then lowered herself into the driver's seat on the right side of the car. The top of her head barely peeked above the low windshield, but she kept her hair short partly to avoid dreadful post-adventure tangles.

Her first experience driving a Morgan with the top down in England taught her that painful lesson.

The seat itself, the wooden knob of the gearshift, everything about the car fit as if it had been designed for her, far more so than the first one across the Atlantic. Even the mirrors were set perfectly.

Ella pushed in the clutch and the brake and started the motor, closing her eyes at the bass rumble.

Barely tamed thunder waiting for her command.

She looked up at Jack's beaming face and smiled.

"I don't think enjoying the day will be a problem."

Chapter 3

ONCE ELLA FOUND the exit sign for course number eight, she left both her day-to-day worries and the constant running dialogue in her head behind.

And fell into her familiar and ever-new groove of merging herself with a driving machine worth abandoning everything else, at least for a little while.

The next two hours were pure joy.

Pure elation.

Pure *acceleration*.

Fresh springtime air and a quick gearshift.

Smooth black pavement cutting through newly born green.

Tight curves and awe-inspiring vistas that successfully tempted her to stop.

Her skin warming and cooling as she constantly passed through shade and sunlight.

With every break, she took the time to drink water for her wind-parched throat, and read about what natural wonders revealed themselves only for her that day.

Towering, jagged ridge lines with more glittering rock than vegetation. A sheer drop-off to a river so far below all she could see was the sun reflecting off the water. Hawks soaring overhead as they began the long migration north.

All with that intoxicating, sweet aroma of the forest coming to life all around her.

A quick glance at the GPS to see what kind of terrain was ahead, and she was off to the next stretch of the joyride.

Her expectation of enjoying the Morgan's road-gripping handling more than the raw power under that long hood proved accurate, without a straight enough stretch of road to put the motor through its paces. And not much chance of one in such a mountainous setting.

She'd just decided to ask Jack about the other courses for tomorrow when the chance opened up right in front of her. A stretch of open road as far as she could see, with pink-budded trees growing far enough back that the whole thing was in sunlight.

Ella glanced down at the GPS, then scowled at the way it flickered.

Between the 2-D electronic version of a road ahead full of gentle curves, and that enticing straightaway.

She'd seen older models do that years ago, getting confused about which route she was on and shifting until they got themselves oriented.

Maybe the mountains interfered just enough with satellite reception in this spot.

Then the screen stayed solid with what her eyes showed.

Ella downshifted and hit the gas.

She didn't get anywhere near typical highway speeds, or even in the neighborhood of what the big engine in the lightweight car could do. But her heart pounded with fierce excitement by the time she backed off for the next slow curve.

What she saw ahead nearly had her hitting the brakes, hard.

Where she'd expected another graceful stretch of hillside—perhaps covered with a stand of proud, tall oaks that wouldn't even consider putting out leaves for weeks—a finely manicured lawn opened up in a gentle climb.

A low rock wall ran unbroken between the lawn and the road, and a house made of the same stone waited in the distance as if it had grown there. Nowhere near as big as the lodge where Jacob was probably deep into his book in front of the fire by now.

But too large to be a private home.

A gap in the rock wall got what was left of Ella's attention, along with the driveway that split away from the road.

Another glance at the GPS—flicker-free for now—showed the driveway led to Paradise Mountain. A destination that hadn't been on her maps or any of the brochures or websites she'd ever seen.

Ella hesitated for only a second, not quite long enough for her momentum to carry her past her chance.

Then she turned the steering wheel to the right and followed the driveway.

The house had a long porch out front, painted white and full of tables and chairs. Several of them occupied. Same with the sides of the driveway as it wound gracefully through masses of the same daffodils and tulips as at the lodge.

Except these were intense violet, brilliant red, and gold bright enough to rival the sun.

Parked alongside the road were what Ella recognized as cars as intensely desired and loved as her Morgan.

She spotted a burly blue Mustang from the Seventies and a scoop-sided white Corvette convertible from the Fifties, tucked right next to sleek black Porsche that looked brand new and a little open-cockpit barchetta the perfect shade of cherry red. A silver, torpedo-shaped Mercedes that looked like it would go like the devil sat off to the side by itself.

Another glance at the GPS showed the checkered black and white flag at the end of the driveway, as if Ella had entered this strange place as her destination before she left the lodge.

A destination that as far as she knew hadn't existed until she saw it on the GPS's little rectangular screen.

"What the hell?" she said under her breath as she parked in front of the Mercedes. "Well, I can't leave without trying to figure it out now."

A man who looked like a younger version of Jack Hughes—the man who'd handed her the Morgan's keys back at the horse barn garage—walked from the broad porch toward her. He wore jeans as well, but instead of a coat with Road to Paradise Mountain on it, his simply said Paradise Mountain with an image of the lodge. His hair was thick and black under his houndstooth cap.

"Welcome!" he said, his English accent quite a bit stronger. "I expect you're a bit confused about what's happened and how you got here. Have a bit of tea to help clear your head."

Ella finally noticed he carried a big white mug, like an oversized teacup. She accepted it because she couldn't get her mind to serve up anything else to do.

The sweet, citrusy aroma of Earl Grey got her dry mouth watering.

A steaming hot sip of the strong, smooth brew forced her brain back into gear, even though she was pretty sure she'd left her normal mental transmission behind.

"Please tell me your name isn't Jack."

The man chuckled and shook his head, even though the resemblance was startling up close.

"No, not I, though I do know him quite well. My name is William. And you are?"

"Well, I was Ella Weaver when I woke up this morning, and when I got behind the wheel of this car. Right now I'm not so sure."

William stepped over to the Morgan and ran a gentle hand along the muscular curve of the long front fender.

"I'm always glad to see this one," he said. "Such a beauty on the outside, with a fierce beast underneath. I'm pleased to meet you, Ella. And to welcome you to Paradise Mountain."

Ella took another long drink of the tea, taking the chance to get a closer look at the house. The handful of people on the porch were laughing and smiling, enjoying what looked (and smelled) like a fine lunch.

She hadn't realized until that moment how much of an appetite her drive had worked up.

"I'm not sure I understand, William. The resort

I've been staying at is the Road to Paradise Mountain. Is this part of that? And how *did* I get here?"

He held up one slender hand and tilted it back and forth. His skin and fingernails were as clean as Jack's had been, but Ella still had the clear impression that he'd know exactly what he was doing under the hood of any of these cars.

"This is part of the resort you came from, and you must indeed travel from there to get here. But not everyone will find the road you did. The one that brings you to our driveway. May I offer you refreshment? Perhaps lunch after your drive?"

Ella shook her head before she could think, and her stomach's irritated grumbling made no difference. She wasn't about to get comfortable here until she knew more *about* here.

"I don't think so, thank you. Maybe I'll come back with my husband tomorrow. Or he could take another of the resort's cars and meet me here later."

"Certainly. He's most welcome to accompany you. But I'm sorry to say I doubt he'd be able to find his way here alone."

Ella finished her tea, and she didn't protest when William reached for the empty mug.

"I don't understand," she said. "Why couldn't Jacob get here on his own?"

William held out one hand toward the lawn.

"Would you care to walk with me? To see more of the grounds?"

"No thank you. I'm comfortable here."

She didn't want to admit it, but Ella was afraid to let the Morgan out of her sight.

He nodded once. "Very well. I hope you won't mind answering a question for me, Ella. Why did you want to come to the resort? I don't believe it was a desire for sheer speed."

Ella raised her eyebrows and shook her head. She'd never quite managed to put that rush, that need that made her want to get in a fantastic car and *go*.

"No, I can get speed in a bunch of different places. One of the best in the world isn't far from here in Virginia. But there's more to it than that, isn't there? More than the twists and turns. What I wanted was...the adventure. The discovery of what's around every new turn."

She turned and looked at the Morgan, at the shape so like a sleek creature getting ready to spring into motion.

"And getting myself there under my own power, in a way, that's part of it. Different than flying, or hiking or riding a bicycle, or a motorcycle, even, at least for me. The way I feel almost *merged* with the car. With the road. I respond to the road and the car responds to me. Does that make any sense outside my own head?"

She looked back at William, knowing a blush was climbing from her chest to her throat and unable to do a thing to stop it.

He closed his eyes and sighed, and when he looked back at Ella, the afternoon sunlight seemed concentrated in his face.

"That makes absolute sense to me. Now tell me, Ella, would your Jacob say the same?"

She smiled and shook her head, rubbing her plain gold wedding band with her thumb.

"No, not Jacob. His idea of a perfect day is quite a bit more stationery. But he wants to come with me tomorrow. Will we have to come the same way? On course number eight? It is a beautiful drive."

William shrugged. "That is entirely up to you. Once you find your way here to Paradise Mountain, you'll always be able to find your way back again. Every course away from the resort will work, as will a select number of perfect drives from all over the world. The only challenge you'll find is you must come back to Paradise Mountain, to this house, before you can get back to the resort."

Ella scowled before she could stop herself. She leaned into the car to get the stack of maps.

"Doesn't this go on to the rest of course eight? It loops back around, that's what I saw on the maps." She shook her head then, looking at the others cars parked around her. "But that doesn't make sense, does it? I didn't see any of these on the road on the way here. And it's supposed to be a closed course."

My own private motorway.

"You've hit upon it now," William said. "If you continue on the way you were going, you'll come to a choice point. An intersection, if you will. You can indeed loop back toward course eight and the resort and Jacob. And everyone else here can do the same, to wherever they came from. Or, you can go on. For a much, much longer drive."

Ella's skin tingled with more than the feel of the cooling afternoon breeze could account for.

This was the electric sense of possibility.

"Where can I go?" she whispered.

"All in good time. For now, let me simply say these roads are only limited by where you *want* to go. And what you can imagine. Time itself need be no limitation to you now that you know the way." He reached out and touched her shoulder for a quick second, and all at once, Ella felt like she'd known him, and Jack, all her life.

It had only taken her a while to find her way to Paradise Mountain so they could meet for the first time.

"Now tell me," he said, "do you believe I'll see you here again tomorrow? And in the future? I would certainly like to."

Ella took in the house and all the people she hadn't spoken to, yet. All of them apparently possessed of the same passion for adventure.

For the *drive*.

And she couldn't imagine a time when she wouldn't want to come back to Paradise Mountain.

"Oh, you'll see me again, William. Tomorrow is only the beginning."

KARI KILGORE

AUTHOR OF THE EARWORMS AND REFLECTIONS

Amy in Wonderland

To Mom

*For an unforgettable night
at the Lyric with Alice*

and so much more

AMY IN WONDERLAND

Amy Holbrook couldn't remember exactly what the marquee for the Lyric Theater looked like when she was five years old.

But judging by photos she'd seen—and more importantly, by the reactions of people old enough to have their own clear memories—the little Appalachian mountain town of Estonoa, Virginia, had done a fantastic job with the restoration.

The old-fashioned three-sided sign glowed with orange and yellow lights all around, contrasting wonderfully with the theater's two stories of red brick scrubbed clean. The bright white space for letters looked almost like a lined notebook, with red letters announcing the Flashback Friday Feature of the week: *Alice's Adventures in Wonderland*.

The live-action version from the early Seventies, too, not the cartoon, with a trivia-worthy glimpse of Dudley Moore as the Dormouse and Peter Sellers as the March Hare. The kind of movie obscure to a whole lot of people, but deeply loved by the passionate few.

Amy was very much on the passionate side.

Thank goodness enough people who lived in Estonoa back then had fond memories of the extra-special showings. Bringing it back to the restored Lyric was an easy choice.

Amy also hadn't been the only one heartbroken when the original marquee collapsed a few years back after over thirty years of neglect. The boxy building with so much magic inside had sat empty and abandoned since the Lyric closed in the late Eighties. She didn't try to hide how seeing it restored better than new now, and knowing everything inside was finally in the same condition, brought a joyful tear to her eye.

Even with all that old-school movie palace glory, her favorite part stood out proud above the marquee. Another red sign jutted out toward the street, with only two sides so you couldn't read it head on. Stylized yellow letters simply said "Lyric," accented by groovy lines top and bottom.

One word could say so much when it was freshly restored and lit up for all the world to see.

An honest-to-goodness box office once again protruded onto the sidewalk, with an Art Deco-style sign for "Tickets" lit up at the top. The crystal-clear glass window sported a circular slotted opening for speaking and a half-circle window at the bottom for exchanging money for a ticket to escape. The window also revealed a beaming ticket seller inside.

For these special nostalgia-laced Fridays, the Lyric brought in someone who'd worked there back in the glory days. Tonight one of the town's most enthusiastic historians had the place of honor.

Sophie Wallace-Robinson wore a smart burgundy jacket that matched the curtains inside, accented with black buttons and the same warm orange as the signs overhead. An adorable little round hat perched at a jaunty angle atop her swirls of silver curls.

A portrait-sized black-and-white photo was tucked up against the glass beside the printed schedule of upcoming movies. A teenaged Sophie with the same uniform, the same grin, much darker hair, and sporting Fifties-Fabulous cat-eye glasses that Amy wished she had herself.

Even people who were only walking by on the inclined sidewalk rather than going inside for the movie waved and greeted Sophie, getting an enthusiastic grin in return. And a lot of folks were out strolling on a beautiful early May evening, enjoying temperatures warm enough for short sleeves but not yet sultry summertime humid.

Several chatted with Sophie on their way into the newly opened Lyric Shoppe just to the right of the theater lobby for dinner, or a quick snack before the movie. Amy's stomach growled at the aroma of hamburgers, fries, and pepperoni pizza that drifted across the street every time someone opened the door.

But tonight she was saving room for Coke and popcorn, and making a nostalgic exception for extra butter.

No need to adhere to the dietary realities of her early fifties when she was celebrating a trip back in time. All the way to her pre-school self, before

Reagan, when disco and even Star Wars hadn't yet entered the world.

She'd even brought out the closest thing she could find to bellbottom jeans to go with a loose-fitting tunic with boxy, geometric shapes in brown, yellow, and green. Her brunette hair wasn't quite long enough to braid or put into two ponytails, so she'd settled for fluffing it out much more than usual.

Amy heard the door of the bookstore she stood in front of open with a cheery jingle, releasing the aroma of paper and fresh coffee, and without looking she knew her best friend Shaun had elbowed his way out with his usual giant haul of books. Sure enough, he carried a stuffed-full huge forest-green canvas bag with *Clinch River Books and Tourist Information* printed in a leaf-like font. A twisting streak of blue ran across the background, successfully bringing the river itself to mind.

Tonight Shaun was as modern as Amy was throwback, with his skinny jeans (that he actually looked great in) and a plain black t-shirt that fit him every bit as well.

"Decide not to go in after all?" he said, settling the bag on the sidewalk between them.

"I wouldn't miss it for anything in the world. Just taking it all in, you know?"

Shaun crossed his arms and stared at the Lyric.

"Want company? I know it's a pretty important memory for you, so I promise to be quiet if you just want someone there with you."

She playfully shoved him with her elbow.

"You know I appreciate the offer, Shaun, but I can't even imagine you sitting quietly through any movie. Especially not a live-action musical of a kids' book."

He shrugged and flashed his generally successful you-love-me-anyway grin.

"It's not my normal jam, no. I swing wildly between over-the-top action flicks and cerebral, moody art house films. I'd go for you, though, and do my very best."

Amy leaned her head on his shoulder for a quick second, then stood up straight and squared her shoulders.

"This is one I should see on the big screen on my own, I think. But I'd be happy to show you my old DVD copy sometime, so I can pause and let you comment and chatter. You'll love the dreamy John Barry score. Very romantic, with a tiny bit of a James Bond echo. This Alice even grew up to be a Bond Girl. Call you later?"

He picked up his bag with a grunt, then leaned in with a raised eyebrow.

"If it's Bond, I'm in. Listen, you'd better call me if you get a dose of the melancholy variety nostalgia, hear? I'd better not find out you moped by yourself. Not when we've shared *so* much high-quality moping time over the years."

"You got it."

Amy watched as he settled into his little green car, blew her a kiss, and drove off before she checked both ways and started across the street. The crowd in the lobby of the Lyric had cleared out a bit, but a bunch of children lingered in one corner.

Just as Amy got to the curb, the kids parted enough for her to see a startlingly realistic White Rabbit, complete with brown tweed suit and twitching whiskers. The Mad Hatter with his top-heavy top hat stood nearby, alongside Tweedledum and Tweedledee with their matching round faces and big bellies. The most remarkable and detailed costume had to be the pointy-headed Caterpillar perched on his mushroom in the corner, massive and elaborately jeweled hookah smoking away by his side.

The kids were understandably enchanted.

But what made Amy nearly trip on the curb was the girl with long, honey blonde hair. Her blue dress with a white apron matched the version from the movie perfectly, all the way down to the little white collar and pink belt.

The resemblance was breathtaking.

If Amy didn't know Fiona Fullerton had played Alice nearly fifty years ago, she would have sworn the Lyric had somehow convinced her to drop by their tiny little Appalachian town just for the night.

And she might have sworn she'd stepped back in time rather than across the street.

She shook herself and kept going, stopping by the box office even though she'd bought her ticket weeks ago when the event was announced. Sophie reached through the little half-circle opening to grasp Amy's hand.

"Amy, so glad to see you! I knew you wouldn't miss our special showing of *Alice*."

Amy nodded and managed to squeeze back.

"I've been looking forward to it for weeks. I saw it when I was five, with my foster mom. They made a pretty big deal of it for us kids."

Sophie grinned. "I was there that night, sitting right here in this booth. Can you believe we were able to get all these wonderful actors from the theatre over in Hidden Springs? I'm sure you remember seeing the group we had the first time. Some of the kids loved it so much they cried when it was over. But I have to say the costumes are *so* much better than before."

Amy kept her own memory to herself.

She was pretty sure she'd been the *only* kid to cry when the magical night ended all those years ago. But in her mind, she saw exactly how the theater lobby and the street outside looked through her tear-blurred, five-year-old eyes.

"I don't remember a whole lot from that night," she fibbed, "but I do remember the actors being here, and how much I loved the movie. This is kind of like stepping back in time."

"Through the looking glass, you mean," Sophie said with a wink. "You know, your foster parents truly were angels. Dan and Bev took in so many and helped you all get through hard times and troubles. Just you and Bev that night on a movie date?"

Amy smiled and nodded, glad the years passing had turned thoughts of her foster parents happy again, rather than the sad overtones right after they died.

"Just the two of us. That's probably why I remember it so clearly. There were a bunch of us, but both of them always made sure each of us had times where we could feel special."

"Well, you'll feel plenty special tonight, then. We got to see a sneak peek earlier today, and you're not going to believe how bright and clear the movie looks now. Better than brand new. You know where your seat is, hon?"

Amy held up her ticket and nodded once. The Lyric always did reserved seating for events like this, and she'd never been more grateful to be able to choose.

"Sure do. Right in the middle of the balcony, front row. Exactly where we sat the first time."

Just then, the White Rabbit opened the door and poked his amazingly lifelike head out. Amy wouldn't be surprised if he simply shed his jacket and pants later on and took himself down to the river, getting smaller with each hop. Eventually ending up small enough to blend in with the ordinary rabbits and adding a rather unpredictable element to their gene pool.

"No time to say hello, goodbye, my dear," he said in a low singsong voice, with a bit of an unnerving grin. "You're late, you're late, you're late."

Sophie giggled and shoed Amy away with both hands.

"Go, go, have a wonderful time."

Amy stepped through the door the White Rabbit held, and she found herself bobbing down into a passable imitation of a curtsey as she passed by for some bizarre reason. Up close, she couldn't see a trace of makeup on his white face, or how his constantly twitching whiskers could possibly be attached.

"*Do* be sure and enjoy your refreshments," he purred. "We made them especially for you."

Amy nodded without looking back. Even though her stomach loudly demanded the promised popcorn now that the scent was thick in the air, she headed toward the burgundy velvet curtain leading to the auditorium rather than to the snack bar. She had no desire to get too close to any of the other actors.

And she was afraid if she looked Alice in the eye she'd burst into tears.

Unfortunately Tweedledum and Tweedledee had relocated themselves to either side of the entrance, and they each held a silvery tray.

Amy wasn't at all surprised to see one held tiny little glass bottles with pinkish liquid inside. A stiff, white paper label attached to the neck said "Drink me." The other tray held a collection of single-bite-sized blue cakes with "Eat me" in pink letters.

"You remember the correct order for such things, don't you?" Tweedledum and Tweedledee said in unison. "Ever so important to take care."

Amy blinked and nodded, taking one of each only because she couldn't think of a way to say no.

Sophie was right. These actors and their costumes were amazing, enough so that she felt a little disoriented.

She was relieved when they trooped in step back across the lobby, waddling gently from side to side.

"Curiouser and curiouser," she whispered to herself.

On a whim she hoped she wouldn't regret but didn't exactly want to resist, she slipped the cake into one of her tunic's huge pockets, then pulled the pinkie-sized cork out of the bottle. She swallowed the whole thing before she could talk herself out of it.

She couldn't exactly say the drink had the dizzying array of savory-sweet, candy-meat flavors as the one in the book, but the strawberry and mint combination was quite pleasant.

She didn't wish to shrink like a telescope, or to be

that sometimes scared and lonely little girl again, the one who'd been so enchanted with the movie and meeting Alice face-to-face.

Her foster parents had been wonderful, and the special nights with each of them meant the world to her, then and now.

But what Sophie didn't know was how tired Amy's foster mom Bev had been that night. A new little girl had arrived a couple of days before: one who needed the consistent attention and reassurance both Bev and Dan were so gifted at providing. No one in the house had been sleeping much.

The movie date happened, yes. But Amy's foster mother slept through almost all of it. A much-needed rest during a stressful time.

Maybe Amy's best, safest wish would be that this night would be as magical as the first one. Even if she knew that wish couldn't possibly come true.

She shook her head and stepped through the velvet curtains.

She'd been inside the little passage many times since the Lyric reopened, so she knew without a doubt that the reddish glow came from dimly lit signs overhead. One pointing the way to the main auditorium to the right, the other left to the balcony stairs.

But she couldn't quite rid herself of the impression of the smiling Cheshire Cat's eyes floating just above her head.

She half-jokingly wondered if she'd shrink as she climbed, a few inches for every step downlit with a rainbow of different colored lights. But the handrail stayed in the same place rather than seeming to get higher as she went.

What changed was the *smells*.

Rather than fresh popcorn and the faint lingering scent of citrus carpet cleaner, she caught a whiff of...cigarette smoke? And sweetish traces of something the Caterpillar might very well have been smoking in his sparkling hookah.

The aroma from the carpet shifted too, away from recently cleaned toward dusty, with a hint of mildew from feet tracking in rain and mud.

Amy paused at the top, her fingertips on the velvet curtain she'd step through onto the balcony. She could easily turn right back around, and do her best to dodge through the lobby before any of the characters caught her and dragged her trembling before the Red Queen.

She had a deep certainty that once she stepped back onto the angled street outside, she'd be in modern-day Estonoa again. Full of smartphones and home theaters, and decades past the days when anyone could smoke inside any building, much less a theater during a movie meant for kids.

She could call Shaun and head right over to his house, where they'd put in her copy of *Alice's Adventures in Wonderland* and watch it on his spectacular, huge television, muddy DVD transfer and all. Chalk it all up to how hard she'd built up this night in her mind, how much she'd looked forward to it.

All that on top of memories of seeing the movie all those years ago that somehow intensified even as they faded.

But then she'd always wonder what might have happened, assuming anything was going to happen at all besides some kind of weird reaction to a sweetened drink on a hungry stomach.

Amy had developed a distaste for wondering what might have been when she was still the little girl who'd watched *Alice*, enchanted, from this very same balcony.

She pushed the curtain aside and stepped through...

...into the early 1970s, small-town Appalachia-style.

The balcony was only five rows deep, and the house lights hadn't gone down for the movie just yet. So she could see way too much to pretend she was mistaken or imagining things.

All the women's hairdos were either beehive tall or parted-down-the-middle straight. The few men either sported what she'd always thought of as aggressive buzz-cuts or slicked-back 'dos shiny with hair cream. Many of the shirts had a distinctive polyester sheen, with lapels that seemed to go all the way to the shoulders.

She was surprised by the number of people of all ages wearing glasses, until she realized contact lenses couldn't have been all that common.

For a second she thought every seat was filled, and that she'd end up crouching on the steps, which would be a perfectly reasonable place for dealing with the odd, floating sensation in her middle and her stunned, barely functioning brain. Possibly caused by slow-moving shock, or mild hyperventilation.

Or she could wander half-dazed back downstairs to see if she emerged back in her own post-2000 time.

But one spot was empty, exactly where Amy knew it had to be.

The middle of the first row of the balcony.

Right beside a girl so small her head barely peeked over the back of her seat, who in turn sat beside an impressively beehived woman who already had her eyes closed and her head leaned back against her own seat.

Amy's feet moved without consulting her, carrying her down a few steps until she stood level with the first row. She felt too tall as she walked, as if her legs were twenty feet long and her head wasn't properly tethered by gravity anymore. Losing her balance and toppling over the edge of the balcony felt like an all-too-real possibility.

Everyone moved, and she only collided with a couple of knees on the way to her own seat.

The one she'd reserved either weeks or decades ago.

Right beside a five-year-old girl sitting with her exhausted foster mother.

A girl with the exact same shade of honey blonde hair as the Alice downstairs, and the one who would soon light up the screen. That girl was years away from her hair darkening to Amy's brunette.

She looked up into Amy's eyes and a brilliant smile shaped her soft, rounded cheeks.

"How did *you* get here?" she said in her high, sweet little girl voice.

"I don't really know. But I sure am glad to see you."

"Will you watch the movie with me?"

Amy somehow managed to sit rather than falling into her seat despite the weakness in her legs. She smiled back at the girl and nodded.

"I'll be right here the whole time. I just *know* we're both going to love it."

The lights overhead slowly dimmed, and a general happy chatter rose and fell all around them. Amy barely had time to wonder which version they'd see—the original one on film, often scratched and fluttery after traveling from theater to theater, or a crisp, newly restored digital print—before the ethereal flutes and strings kicked in.

As soon as she saw the whimsical rounded, flowery frame with the opening credits inside, Amy gasped. The green background was sharp and clear, and the delicate drawings that changed as the credits rolled looked fresh and brand new.

She heard other young children around them whispering, impatient for the words to go away so the story could start. She knew without looking that the little girl beside her wasn't one of them.

When Amy did look, the girl stared rapt at the screen, still smiling. Turning her head ever so slightly from one side to the other, trying to capture every note of the beautiful music. Capturing it so deeply and so well that not only the music but the way it *felt* would linger in her mind and her heart for half a century.

All at once, Amy remembered one of the songs, in fact the last song in the movie, was called "The Me I Never Knew."

The air left her lungs just as the screen shifted to bright sunshine and a boat on a lake.

She had no idea which one of her selves the song had been meant for: the woman or the little girl.

But Amy knew what a tremendous gift this night would be for both of them.

She took in a deep, slow breath, and relaxed into

her seat, refusing to question how or especially why she'd gotten here. She *was* here, not once but twice.

And she intended to enjoy every minute.

She watched her younger self as much as the movie, fascinated by every feature and changing expression. About halfway through, the little girl scooted over to the side of her seat, leaning her head on Amy's arm.

After a few seconds, Amy put her arm around the girl's shoulders, marveling at how reality and memory moved into alignment. She'd long thought her step-mother stirred during the movie, and that was who she'd sat close with.

Maybe that had happened, too.

Now, in this precious timeline or warp or what-ever it was, she treasured being the source of comfort for a child who'd needed it so badly. And who would remember it so fondly.

As the last song started, "The Me I Never Knew," the little girl looked up at Amy again. This time with a serious expression that didn't fit her tiny young face.

"Do you have to go now?"

Amy closed her eyes, fighting back the urge to say of course not. She'd stay here forever, or maybe even try to take both of them back to her future. Take this child in and give her all the love and affection she could possibly ever need.

When she opened her eyes, she was looking right at Bev.

Still taking the so badly needed rest that she could have gotten at home, because she wanted to make sure little-girl-Amy had a special night.

Bev, who along with Dan, had given Amy and all

the other children they cared for so much. Love and affection and confidence and courage, and a thousand tiny things Amy couldn't put into words.

She didn't have to. They were part of her.

Depriving her five-year-old self of that childhood, that incredible joy-filled life, would be an awful disservice.

A mistake she'd never make.

"I'm sorry, sweetheart," she said. "You're right. I do have to go. But I'll remember this night forever, won't you?"

Her smaller self nodded, lips pressed together and faint eyebrows drawn down. Trying so, so hard not to cry.

"I'll remember. But I don't *want* it to be over. I want to stay right here with you, and see the movie, and hear the music. I never loved anything so much that it *hurt*."

Amy let out a half-sob, half-laugh, and leaned over to hug the sweet little girl tight.

"I think I understand how you feel. Because I love *you* so much it hurts."

The little girl shook her head against Amy's arm.

"Then don't go."

Amy sat back and lowered her face so she could look into her own eyes, lashes wet with tears.

"You know who else loves you so much it hurts? Dan does, and Bev does, too. They'll take such good care of you. You're going to grow up to be so happy."

The little girl nodded, but her chin still trembled.

Doing everything she could to be brave.

"Promise?"

Amy smiled and stroked the girl's soft cheek. The

song was almost over, and people started to stir and shift around them.

They were almost out of time.

"I promise. Thank you for watching the movie with me. Don't forget to tell Bev how much you loved it."

"I won't forget. I can't tell her about you."

"Probably not. It's okay. Maybe we'll see each other again someday. I can't promise on that one. But I hope so."

The lights slowly came up.

The little girl stood and threw her arms around Amy's neck, all silky hair and warm breath and smelling of strawberry shampoo.

"I hope so too," she whispered.

She turned back just as Bev sat up and stretched her arms out to the front, then smiled.

"What did you think of the movie, Amy?"

Amy's heart broke within her then, when she realized she couldn't talk to her step-mother again no matter how much she'd always wanted to. Just like the one-on-one movie date, this night had been about the little girl, not the grownups. At least *more* about the little girl.

"I loved it all so much," the little girl said, her voice watery with tears.

Bev frowned and reached for the tissues she always and forever had stowed in one of her pockets.

"What's wrong, then, honey? Why are you crying?"

The little girl hesitated for a second, her small shoulders hitching, once, twice.

"Because I never wanted it to be over."

Bev smiled again, and pulled the little girl close.

"Then it must have been *wonderful*."

Bev looked into Amy's eyes and smiled.

Amy managed to smile back, but she had to get out of there before she was the one crying enough to flood the whole theater, just like Alice had flooded the hallway. The last thing she wanted was to intrude on this special moment between her younger self and Bev, or cause a scene by trying to push past everyone to get away.

All at once, she knew what she had to do.

She stood, reaching into her tunic pocket. Not for tissues she really should have been keeping for herself.

She drew out the tiny little cake with "Eat Me" written on it. When Bev focused on her little girl again, Amy popped the cake into her mouth. An explosion of tart currents and sweet, spicy cake spread throughout her whole body.

Thank goodness she didn't grow, getting taller and taller until her elbows and knees took up every bit of the whole theater, trapping everyone inside.

Instead she felt...lighter. More like a fluffy cloud than a woman. Not quite like she could pass through the walls themselves. But she had a feeling she'd pass through the crowd without causing any sort of disruption.

She glanced back at Bev and her younger self one more time. Five-year-old Amy still spoke through tears as Bev gathered their things. But she was saying all the things she loved about *Alice's Adventures in Wonderland*.

From what she overheard, and what she remembered, Bev was getting a retelling nearly detailed enough that she'd recognize every scene and line of dialog when she finally saw the movie for herself. Foreshadowing Amy's easy ability to store away incredible amounts of detail about anything she loved enough to pay close attention to.

Amy turned and walked away, so the little girl wouldn't be so terribly tempted to point her out to Bev after all.

Her feet felt like they never touched the ground all the way downstairs toward the lobby. And she never in a million years would have thought she'd feel melancholy when the ghostly aroma of cigarettes faded, giving way to carpet cleaner by the time she reached the ground floor.

Not the sort of melancholy Shaun meant when he insisted she call him if the evening left her upset. She'd call to reassure him, and certainly join him for that *Alice* movie date someday.

But this was the kind of melancholy she would keep entirely between the two parts of herself, just as she'd done most of her life.

A treasure far more sweet than bitter.

She hesitated at the final velvet curtain, only then realizing the crowd around her had dissipated somehow. She stood alone, with ordinary signs overhead rather than a Cheshire Cat grin.

Maybe none of it had happened at all except inside her own imagination.

The truth was that didn't matter, not really. Amy knew the memory of the precious connection, her little-girl-self's warmth and trust, would linger.

Exactly the same way her own memory of that magical night in Wonderland had lingered for her all these years later.

When she stepped into the lobby—where adults

and children gathered around the costumed actors with gray-haired Sophie, still in her jaunty ticket-selling uniform—the White Rabbit waited only for her.

"Was I on time?" she said, repeating her curtsey.

He stared into her eyes for an endless moment, whiskers twitching.

Then he smiled.

"You were always in exactly the right place, in exactly the right time."

He bowed low, sweeping his gloves and fan toward the front door.

For the second time as she passed through, Amy saw the street outside the Lyric Theater through a haze of joyful tears.

The Lightning-Struck Wood

For friends I wish I could talk to

one more time

THE LIGHTNING -
STRUCK WOOD

PAUL MURRAY always thought it was people that made a house feel like a home.

Especially at his best friend Sadie's house.

Even now, at the end of what most people would have considered a sad occasion, a handful of Paul's closest friends in the world lingered in the cozy living room. The last loyal holdouts from crowds that had passed through all day long, paying their respects.

Sprawled across two hand-made sofas, with simple wooden arms made from a tree downed in a long-ago lightning strike. Years after they were sewn and stuffed, the paisley fabric cushions were still far more comfortable than anything from a factory.

Reclining on huge matching beanbag chairs, large enough that Paul had slept there on several occasions after late-night talks. Or even sitting cross-legged on thick braided rag rugs scattered around the ancient hardwood floor, close enough to the workhorse black wood stove that kept the whole house comfortable on the coldest winter nights.

Like this one in the melancholy depths of January.

When the deep-freeze outside made Paul's bones ache, and the dry air inside made what was left of his brown hair hopelessly staticky. A cast-iron pot of water on the stove and a big humidifier helped, but the season couldn't be so easily tamed.

He tried his best to convince himself he wasn't still smelling Sadie's soft patchouli perfume in the air a year and a day after her passing.

No, that had to be something in her special recipe herb-covered popcorn they'd consumed massive amounts of during this all-day living memorial.

Between all those glorious, butter-covered carbo-hydrates and a few bottles of apple cider balanced perfectly between sweet and dry, he figured a bit of light-headed nostalgia was forgivable.

Every square inch of the rustic-charming house was a nostalgia overdose on days like this when he slowed down enough to pay attention. He knew each dark beam along the ceiling and walls, and every colorful stone of the wood stove's elevated hearth.

He'd helped hang each framed people- or nature-filled photograph and painting. Several of the photos had come from his ever-evolving cameras: starting with simple hand-cranked versions back in the Seventies through complicated and expensive Nineties models with lenses and a hundred adjustments, all the way to the smartphone in his pocket.

He and Sadie had researched and saved until they could afford a high-end photo printer to handle the output of the digital revolution, hidden away in the cramped office with the computer. Digital photo frames simple wouldn't do.

She always wanted things she could touch and hold on to.

He'd read all the books on the rough-edged wooden shelves, helped dust the vast collections of pretty rocks and bird feathers and hand-carved wooden trinkets tucked in between.

The many battered and wounded souls who'd passed through this house brought their own contributions when they arrived, and often when they returned to say thank you.

Seashells and little statues and travel souvenirs, whatever symbolized how they'd healed and grown and set out confidently into lives of their own.

Sadie never tired of welcoming them back, making sure they never felt guilty for walking through her door bruised and in pain. Her life's work and joy was seeing them thrive in the safe space they needed to recover.

And always, always encouraging them to pass that gift along however they could.

Hell, Paul had been the one to help Sadie move into what was then a mostly abandoned family house a few miles outside of Bountyfield, Virginia, when they were both seniors in high school.

She hadn't brought much then—a pitiful carful of belongings that made Paul's fifty-two-year-old heart ache at the memory. At the time, he'd been mightily impressed at her courage in leaving her home and family before she turned eighteen.

He'd had to grow up and sever plenty of his own ties before he understood what drove her to it.

One of the recipients of Sadie's care and

generosity who'd passed it along countless times stretched and yawned in her spot in front of the wood stove. Gayle looked like she's been born with the courage and confidence to run an at-risk youth advocacy center out in Asheville, with her spiky short red hair, bold metal jewelry, and flowing goddess-like green dress.

She made a real difference for children *much* younger than anyone he and Sadie had ever taken in. The ones too young to even know they could possibly make changes for themselves.

But Paul remembered the terrified eighteen-year-old Gayle who locked herself in one of the upstairs bedrooms for weeks when she arrived twenty years ago. And how Sadie hadn't pushed or pried. She'd only left Gayle's meals outside the door and gave her the time and safety she needed.

He remembered more kids like that than he could ever count.

"I'm sorry to be the first to break the spell," Gayle said, getting gracefully to her feet. "But I've got to head out. We're stopping over on the way instead of driving through, so don't worry about me falling asleep halfway."

Two men and three more women stood when Gayle did, starting the extended sequence of good-byes and hugs before Paul stood to join in. As usual, he waited off to the side, never having fully shed the polite little boy who was told he was to keep himself quiet and out of sight way too often.

The best he'd ever been able to care for that little boy inside was to convince him that Adult Paul would never, ever forget about him.

Or punish him for being too much of a bother.

Gayle worked her way around to him and squeezed him tight enough that his spine crackled. Paul sighed and relaxed into her warmth and strength and soothing lavender fragrance.

Almost like one final, much-needed hug from Sadie.

"I know you've lived up here for a long damn time," Gayle said, stepping back and holding his shoulders, her green eyes staring intently into his, "and I still say I don't like you spending tonight alone. One of us can stay, or better yet, you grab your toothbrush and go on a little vacation with us. The gods know you've earned it."

Paul shook his head before she let go, and her rueful smile let him know she wasn't surprised.

"I appreciate the thought and the invitation, I really do. I'll take you up on that trip to Asheville, if I ever settle back into enough of a routine around here. But this is one of those saying goodbye things, you know? I don't know how many more days and nights I'll have with this old house. Gotta take my chance to visit with Sadie's spirit while I can."

"You already know how I feel about Sadie's family swooping in out of nowhere, trying to run you off when they knew good and god damn *well* she wanted you here, just like her aunt and uncle wanted *her* here. I'm just thankful those assholes couldn't wedge their greedy little fingers into that iron-clad will she had."

Gayle frowned and took her turn to shake her head.

"You deserve this place, Paul, and you're the one to keep it going. No one who ever passed through here will let it come to Sadie's dream ending. We'll help you get all that tax mess sorted out if you just let us."

Paul kissed her cheek and nodded, hoping his smile looked real enough, then repeated the performance for everyone else as they gathered themselves up to go.

Even with the prospect of a lonely night ahead, he breathed a sigh of relief when he closed the rough wooden door.

Sadie had loved telling people how her aunt and uncle had salvaged that and most of the wood inside from the family's original Depression-era house. Bringing everything they could into their new vacation home.

The *new* one that was every minute of fifty years old now. Sadie's desperate escape had saved it from collapsing back into the forested Virginia landscape it came from after years of neglect.

Years after her aunt and uncle took the same steps away from the family that she had, if in less dramatic fashion.

Saved herself from collapsing from neglect, too.

She and Paul and her attorney had correctly (and sadly) predicted the way the so-called family she'd fled so many years ago would swarm out of the ether, wanting to claim and take over the house when she passed. Demonstrating a cold-hearted sense of entitlement to all the hard work of Sadie and countless friends and survivors over the decades.

Paul wasn't sure he'd be able to keep up with maintenance costs after the legal nightmare led to a new real estate assessment, and a big jump in property taxes he dreaded trying to fight.

But he was damn sure proud to have kept the

family vultures from picking over the remains for free.

He set out a big glass of water to chase all that cider, and an envelope he'd gotten from Sadie's attorney a couple of days ago, with today's date on the flap. Then he changed into a pair of old black pajamas, dragged one of the beanbag chairs as close to the wood stove as he safely could, and flopped into it like he had as a much younger man.

There were three bedrooms down here, including his own, and several more he and a bunch of volunteers had helped add on upstairs. Much-needed expansion for young folks who needed a safe place to land when they refused to take abuse any longer, or to get shoved into an ill-fitting role or path in their own lives.

But he fully expected to sleep down here tonight, lulled by the faint roar and crackle of the fire. Not because he was listening to one of those kids who'd finally worked up the courage to tell their story, or working out support strategies with Sadie or the other adults who helped whenever they could.

Tonight, Paul meant to read what he suspected was the last message he'd ever receive from his friend. And he hoped to somehow reach out to her one more time.

He stared into the merrily burning fire through the stove door glass, not exactly missing the old brown Seventies model that stood in that spot when Sadie moved in. She'd somehow managed to coax the temperamental hunk of metal into keeping the place warm, and taught Paul how to fuss and swear and wrangle it into service.

The upstairs addition required an upgrade to the

stove, and the need for better circulation led to the unimaginable luxury of a heat pump and furnace for hot summers and mild winter nights.

Then about five years ago, a well-deserved grant for Sadie's work with survivors of abuse and neglect brought the gleaming black modern beauty keeping Paul's toes and the rest of the house toasty. He and Sadie had giggled and marveled at the tiny little fan that kept soot from building up on the glass, saving them from constant scrubbing.

He held up his glass toward the warmth-giving heart of their home.

"Here's to you, Sadie. I can't begin to count the number of lives you made better. I know mine was one of them. I never could repay you while you were still here. I hope to at least keep passing that gift along as long as I'm still drawing breath."

After a long drink of the cool water, Paul opened the envelope and found exactly what he expected inside: a smaller envelope with his name on the front, in Sadie's scrawling handwriting.

He smiled and blinked back a few unexpected tears, the first in months, before he pulled out the folded pieces of decidedly old-fashioned pink stationery and started to read.

Paul,

I don't know if it was the firestorm in my gut or a random accident that took me out.

Either way, I'm sorry to leave you there alone, my friend. I never would have if I'd had my way.

I hate to guess how much hell my family has put you through over the house and the land. They're experts at stirring it up for damn sure. I don't have to know details to say I'm so, so sorry.

And maybe I can help with part of it.

Do me a favor and start a fire in that gorgeous stove if you haven't already. Then throw just a little more wood on, would you? Not from the usual pile, though.

Grab a couple of sticks from my secret special occasion stash that I kept on top of the shelves by the front door. In the big old wooden box.

Toss them in and wait.

I hope I'm about to show you the only secret I ever kept from you.

Love you, brother,

Sadie

Paul rubbed his damp cheeks, then levered himself out of the chair with only a couple of grunts.

"Anything they put me through was a gentle caress compared to what they did to you," he said under his breath. "But I sure do appreciate the thought."

He stopped in front of the collection of irregularly shaped wooden shelves, all cast-offs from a local lumber mill. They'd saved the leftovers from cutting up a snow-downed tree years ago at Sadie's request. The mill delivered perfectly even half-inch-thick boards, but with widths that curved and varied wildly.

Once he and Sadie had installed them with the uneven sides out, brown edges and all, the shelves looked like they'd grown there. Figuring out what would fit in the whimsical spaces was more than half the fun.

Tucked up against the ceiling was an antique wooden box that so nearly matched the age-darkened color of the walls and shelves that it was easy to overlook. A couple of feet long and about a foot tall, smooth and undecorated.

Paul had watched Sadie climb up on a little stepladder to put it up there the day after the shelves were finished, with the air of someone who didn't want to answer questions.

So that's exactly how he handled it.

He'd never looked inside the box or bugged her about it, not once. He figured when someone so open and honest about every single thing in her life actually wanted to keep a secret, he needed to respect that.

He barely managed to get a good grip on the box without needing to get the ladder himself, and almost staggered back when he realized it was much heavier than it looked.

It was also open on top rather than having any kind of lid, so he got a glimpse inside right away after so many years of never peeking.

The box was full of sticks and twigs, several the two-foot length of the box, most smaller. All of them dry, almost all with rough gray bark a little singed and blackened around the edges. He'd guess oak from the fissures and cracks on the bigger pieces.

Paul settled the box on the floor in front of the stove, then parked himself back in the beanbag chair. He leaned his face in close to get a good sniff.

Dusty, but with a strong undertone of scorched wood.

Frowning, he picked out two sticks about the same width as his fingers and not a whole lot longer. The black soot rubbed off onto his thumb.

If this was from the same long-ago lightning tree

as the sofas, saved all these years, he couldn't imagine why Sadie wanted him to burn it now.

Even if he lived another fifty years himself, he'd never be one to ignore the final request from his best friend.

Paul shifted onto his knees on the brown and green hearth rug, slipping on the leather gloves for tending the stove. When it was roaring hot like this, even opening the door could give his knuckles an unpleasant singe.

He grabbed the bright silvery handle and turned it toward the middle, pulled the door open, then tossed the two sticks in before too much hot air billowed out.

And he sat back and waited.

The dry wood flared up right away, making two brighter lines in the yellow flames and red coals underneath. Before Paul could wonder if the sticks would be part of that bed of coals before anything happened, the clear glass smudged gray.

He scowled and shook his head, then smiled at his own reaction. After decades of working to keep the glass on the old stoves clean, he flashed into irritation every bit as quickly as those sticks had caught. Not all that different from someone (like him) who remembered the distant era of Before Microwave getting annoyed at how long it took to nuke a frozen dinner.

He'd just have to clean the glass in the morning, then check the owner's manual.

Probably nothing more...more than a clogged...

Except the glass wasn't gray any more.

He still couldn't see through to the fire, but now

the smudges were whorls and streaks of the same red and yellow as inside.

Shifting even as he watched to purple and green.

Paul's body froze as solid as the ground outside, but his mind jerked and creaked into overdrive. He had no idea whether to run out the front door to avoid some weird toxin, open the stove door and try to fish the remains of those sticks out, or stay right where he was.

He dragged a deep breath into his lungs and reminded himself why he was doing *any* of this.

"Sadie asked you to, right? And you trust her. So you sit tight. And you wait."

He forced the breath out and gasped in another when the shapes on the glass changed again.

Forming a rough outline of a human face, gradually gaining definition.

Taking on the same tan skin and brown hair as the one he knew so well.

Then Sadie grinned out at him brighter than the hottest coal inside.

He managed to open his mouth, but all the words he'd ever known forgot the way from his brain.

The crackle and roar of the now-unseen fire surged up past the glass, and slowly modulated into a sound Paul thought he'd never hear again.

Sadie saying his name.

"Sadie?" he finally choked out.

"Paul. I'm right here."

"Please tell me that's you and not some kind of hallucination I'm having. Or did you slip something onto those sticks that would get me into trouble with a drug test?"

Sadie's face tilted to the side and now the crackles rose and fell just like laughter.

"I can't say anything about a drug test if you had the party today like you promised. But it's me. As much me as I can manage, and not for very long."

Paul knelt on the hearth rug again, resisting a powerful urge to reach out and touch the rocket-hot glass.

"Should I even ask how? Or just skip to *why*, and when can you come back?"

Sadie nodded, her chin slipping out of view below the edge of the glass.

"*How* is that lighting-struck wood. I discovered it accidentally with the first stove years ago, when I ended up talking to the people who built the very first house here. My great-grandparents. Scared the shit out of me, to be honest. I gathered up every stick and twig I could find from that tree that day. Then after my aunt and uncle passed, I talked to them."

Paul hugged himself, struggling to hold back more questions than he could possibly have time to ask. He couldn't resist one that he'd been worried about since a year and a day ago.

"Are they with you now, Sadie? So you're not alone wherever you are?"

"They're here, and a whole bunch of others. I'm not alone, Paul. But I am lonely for *you*. Let me tell you *why* I wanted to talk to you today before my time runs out. Look at the wall behind the stove, on the right. See a sparkly black rock that looks like it has a letter 'Z' down the middle?"

Paul leaned forward, not wanting to let her out of his sight.

To let *Sadie* out of his sight.

"I see it."

"If you give that rock a good shove on the bottom, it should tip right out. The poker from the stove tools will do it. This is going to seem like something out of an old spy movie, but there's an envelope in there. Not even my lawyer knows about what's inside. She'd probably call me paranoid for all of this, but she didn't grow up with my family."

Paul got to his feet and picked up the poker, holding the handle shaped like an open circle in one hand. He set the pointy end against the rock and pushed, grinning like a little boy when it fell out into his hand.

Sure enough, a plain envelope browned and crinkly with time waited inside.

"What is this?" he said, kneeling again and tearing it open. He held up a squat, barrel-shaped key. "Is this to a safe or something?"

"I knew you'd figure it out," Sadie said, with her warm smile that helped heal so many broken hearts. "That's to a safe deposit box over in Wolf Branch. Let's just say I don't have any family there, so it was worth making the drive. I saved up as much money as I could, and there's a life insurance policy I got when I was twenty-three. The good kind without the fees and junk. It should all be close to a hundred thousand dollars by now."

Paul blinked and sat back, nearly dropping the suddenly precious key.

"How did you manage to keep all of this secret, Sadie? For so long?"

She shook her head, and Paul was startled to notice the outlines of her face were already fading.

"I just... I didn't want any of them to know about

it, Paul. They were awful to me as a kid, and worse the few times I couldn't avoid them as an adult. I'm sorry for how nasty I'm sure they've been to you. I figured this way I could help when everything settled down. When enough time passed that they'll all leave you alone."

Paul nodded, then realized he had no idea whether she could see him or not.

"It will help, more than you know. Enough that I can keep this place going now, the way you wanted it run. And yeah, they gave up on bothering me a while back. I truly hate to ask this, but are you running out of time?"

"I am, and way sooner than I'm ready to. Listen, I know there's not much wood left. But *this* is what it's for. I'm good here, I truly am. Nothing hurts, not any more. Not even my memories hurt now. My biggest worry is how you're doing. If I can help you, even if it's just talking sometimes, that's exactly what I want to do. Okay?"

"Okay," Paul said, holding the key against his heart. "I won't say I'll let you go, because I never did that to start with. But I will ask you one question. What if this hadn't worked, and you couldn't tell me about the key?"

This time when Sadie laughed, he heard the roar all the way up into the chimney, and her image brightened to its full intensity again.

"Well, if you get another letter from my lawyer in a couple of weeks, you'll know what to expect. I wrote the whole thing out just in case. Will the money help, Paul? Will it make a difference?"

This time Paul did reach out toward the glass, stopping before it got uncomfortably hot against his fingers. Sadie's outline faded to purple and green, then toward orange and red.

"It will make all the difference in the world for the kids who need what your house can offer, like you always did. Talking to you makes all the difference to me. Love you, sister."

Her reply was lost in the normal sounds of the fire.

But Paul saw her say "Love you, brother" before her image faded into gray smudges on the glass.

A few seconds later, it was back to its crystal-clear perfection.

He had no idea how long he lingered there, hoping for the faintest ripple or echo that never came.

When he finally stirred, he was thirsty enough to swallow the rest of his water in one go.

The temptation to feed more of the lightning-struck wood into the stove, talking the night away with Sadie as he'd so often done for most of his life, burned strong and deep within him.

He tucked the box back onto the top shelf instead.

As much as he'd learned from her over the years, he had no doubt he'd need her advice to help some heartbroken kid get through the first hours, days, and weeks after escaping a terrible situation. That was worth saving up his time with Sadie for.

Much like she'd made what he hoped were many more years of giving that help possible with everything she'd saved for him.

Paul built up the fire for the night, then curled up to sleep in front of it.

Wondering if he'd have the courage to ask her one more question the next time they talked.

As he closed his eyes, he decided he'd rather find out if he'd make it to wherever Sadie was when it was his time to draw his own final breath.

Until then, he'd keep making her house a home for everyone who needed it.

Including himself.

KARI KILGORE

AUTHOR OF ODDS AND ENDINGS AND THE EARWORMS

A Taste Just Like a Hug

Chapter 1

KAY WALTON LOVED nothing more than making sure people were happy. And her favorite place to do just that was in her own café in the high mountain town of Lightning Gap, Virginia.

Kay's Café sat in the middle of the long main street, tucked in among an amazing variety of lovely old Victorian homes built when the town was founded. Turned out the local prevailing style back in the 1910s and 1920s called for solid craftsmanship, elaborate decoration everywhere it could possibly fit, and a bunch of folks making every eccentric choice they possibly could while they were at it.

To this day, all the residents and shopkeepers carried on that tradition of keeping a good way away from what outsiders might call normal. And the types of people who were either from Lightning Gap or visited and realized that was where they belonged wouldn't stand living any other way.

Some said the long, sheltering ridgeline that seemed to embrace the whole town and keep it safe and protected carried its own variety of peculiar magic that made it feel like home.

Even when the towering Lightning Stone that sat high and proud at the end of that ridge earned the name every time a good storm got going.

Kay felt lucky every single day that she got to walk downstairs in her own stately Victorian home—painted a vibrant gold with accents of robin's egg blue, spring green, and rich pink—and end up in the kitchen of her café. No one knew why the ground floor had been converted with open spaces and broad plate glass windows way back when, but she was thankful for it every single day and night.

No worries about a commute through rain or snow or anything else for her, and she wouldn't have it any other way.

Some of the older folks still grumbled about how she'd renovated the place a few years back, but not a one of them stopped coming in for the best comfort food outside of their own grandmother's house.

And anyway, with the brave new frontier of the year Two Thousand close on the horizon, this hardly seemed the time to cling to the past in such a silly way. After all, Kay knew the value of tradition where it counted better than anyone else for miles around.

In the kitchen and at the table.

Right now the heavenly aroma of fried chicken justified her confidence, along with potatoes and onions getting to know each other in hot cast-iron perfection. Right behind that, the scent of strawberry-rhubarb pie promised to highlight the bountiful springtime harvest at its early season best.

Most of her regulars loved how she'd updated the colors but kept the same classic soda fountain feel.

New Formica tables with shiny chrome around the edges, now in the same warm pink and green as the house, and her favorite cheery robin's-egg blue. She'd carried those exact shades onto the walls, and even the fabulous Fifties-style uniforms she and everyone else wore.

She'd had her custom version of a fluffy full-skirted one for a few years now, but she never tired of the way it swirled out around her knees when she turned fast enough. That was enough to keep her quick on her feet like she was twenty instead of within kissing distance of fifty.

Her big colorful name badge making sure everyone who passed through the door knew they were talking to the proud owner of Kay's Café kept her on her toes.

She could see all the tables and booths from her perch at the end of the soda fountain's bar, with the bonus of getting to watch everything her handsome husband Adam whipped up.

Thick, rich milkshakes in enough flavors to need their own little menu, delicious foamy floats made out of anything fizzy they had on hand, even several varieties of scooped ice cream to go along with the soft serve.

Kay's favorite thing to watch, and to sample, was the endless variation on an ordinary Coke. Cherry and raspberry were naturals, and the most frequent orders. Then folks branched out into vanilla, lemon, lime, chocolate, and even flavors like almond, cinnamon, or pomegranate.

Whenever Kay or any of the other people taking orders brought him an unusual one, Adam always winked, grinned, and got to work.

Kay liked a perfectly drawn original Coca-Cola best herself. The bright bubbles tickling her nose let her know the bittersweet flavor would be just the way she liked it.

Best of all was when a pleasant lull between breakfast and lunch, or lunch and dinner, gave her time to walk around and visit with friends and new arrivals alike. See how they were doing, find out what they might need.

And if she'd ever seen someone who needed her special attention more than her old high school friend Venus Mullins Thompson right then, she couldn't remember a thing about it.

Even though she'd been born, raised, and married right here in the same Appalachian Mountains as Kay, Venus always looked like an exotic creature who'd wandered in from an adventure movie.

Or at least from one of the exciting world trips she and her husband Charlie were always getting ready to leave on or just getting back from.

From the way Venus sat sideways at one of the pink tables, Kay couldn't tell whether the flowing garment she wore was a dress, a skirt and top, or a top and extra-wide pants. But with the silky drape of the deep orange fabric—and the way it seemed to ripple and shift colors like a dancing fire whenever she moved—Kay knew it hadn't come from within a thousand miles of Lightning Gap.

The same had to be said of the copper earrings set with sparking green stones that dangled from Venus's ears, and the matching necklace.

Where Kay's wavy strawberry blonde hair never got past her chin, Venus wore her thick brunette locks more than halfway down her back. Today she had it pulled back into an intricate braid with a twisting design Kay had never seen before. More of the glittering green stones peeked out on a ribbon worked right into the braid.

Even with such a glorious, colorful outfit, and the remains of a bowl of thick, peppery Appalachian soup beans, proper mountain savory cornbread, and fresh spring green onions that should have put a smile on anyone's face, Venus sat with her chin held in one hand. Idly stirring her surely gone-cold drink in its pale green mug and staring into space.

Kay waved Adam over, and her heart jumped up and paid attention as much as it had the first day they met when he smiled and headed her way. Even after not quite thirty years of marriage, her high school sweetheart still perked her up just right. From his curly brown hair and big blue eyes, to his broad shoulders and fine backside.

He leaned in and dropped a quick kiss on her cheek to let her know he felt exactly the same.

"Hey sweet pea," she said. "Do you happen to know what Venus is drinking? I didn't take her order today. One of her fancy teas she brings back from her trips?"

"Nope, not today." He shook his head slowly and frowned. Kay wasn't the only one who'd noticed Venus being down. "That's plain old coffee, *not* that your coffee is ever plain. Best I ever tasted. But I don't think I've ever seen Venus order much of anything to drink without a special request."

Kay nodded. "You're right. Usually whatever she thinks up tastes fantastic, too. Listen, mind to send one of the kids over with a fresh pour for her in a couple minutes? And one of your best-in-the-world Cokes for me?"

"Sure thing, sugar pie. If anyone can figure out what's got Venus feeling droopy, it's you."

This time Kay was the one to wink as she sashayed toward Venus, making sure to give her skirt a flirty twirl for Adam's benefit.

Venus didn't move until Kay was a couple of steps away. Then she sat back and took a deep breath as if she'd gotten startled, or was sitting there half asleep.

"Hey there Kay. I was off gathering nonsense about a million miles away."

Kay pulled out the chair across from Venus and settled herself onto the extra-comfortable cushions. She'd made sure each and every place in the café invited folks to sit and stay a spell, and she loved the way customers always made sure each table had chairs of different colors tucked underneath.

"That's okay, Venus. It's no wonder, with all those travel memories you have stored inside your mind. Planning your next getaway?"

Venus smiled, but it was a sad and pitiful affair.

"Planning a trip, sure. But not to anywhere I'm looking forward to, at least not this time. Charlie's daddy passed away last night. We just got back from spending the last few days with him down there in Estonoa. We'll be heading back over in a couple of days for the funeral."

Kay's heart ached the way it always did when someone right in front of her faced challenging bad times, even if she'd just met them five minutes before.

Knowing Venus all her life made it ever so much worse.

"Oh no, I'm *so* sorry to hear that, hon. Once you've been married for a while, that's the same as losing part of the family you were born to. Is there anything at all we can do for you two, or for his people?"

Adam appeared at her elbow just then, with a big glass of Coca-Cola in one hand and a fresh coffee in the other. Kay smelled a heavy dose of Venus's favorite cinnamon and ginger in a brand-new blue mug with the café's wonderful new Art Deco logo on the side, designed by the senior art class at the Lightning Gap High School.

Adam had it done in secret, just in time for her birthday.

Kay truly had hit the jackpot when it came to marrying time.

"Thought you might like a fresh cup, Venus," he said with that gorgeous smile of his, then he was gone.

Venus wrapped both hands around the mug and took in a deep breath, and her own smile wasn't quite as sad as before.

"Something like this is about the best thing anyone can do," she said. "I sure do appreciate you and Adam taking care of me at a time like this, you know? Just one of those awful things we have to get through, I guess." She took a drink and closed her eyes for a second. "You'll understand this probably better than anyone else I know, with the way you specialize in comfort food and how much it matters and all. It's just so *sad* when someone passes, and they loved making something special that you know you'll never get again."

Kay nodded slowly, remembering all the things she'd been lucky enough to learn from her parents and grandparents and aunts and uncles, and a bunch of people she'd met along the way. Not everyone got that chance to learn, or even if they did, the results never were quite right.

Some mysterious touch of magic—of love made so real you could touch and smell and taste it—passed away from the world.

"What was it your father-in-law made that you loved so well, Venus? I know I probably can't get it right, but I sure would like to try."

Venus laughed under her breath.

"The best thing he ever made was apple pie, if you can believe that. Well, more the filling for it, since he used it in all kinds of different things. Apple crisp and cakes and the cutest little hand pies, and he even put the rehydrated slices in with good fresh greens and such. You could make a whole meal out of one of his salads with those apples and walnuts and crumbled up cheese so sharp it made your jaws ache."

Venus pulled a delicate handkerchief out her pocket (that gorgeous outfit was wide-legged pants and a top after all), made of shimmery black fabric with delicate purple lace all around the edges. Kay patted her hand when she finished blotting her eyes.

"Those dried apple slices sure do come in handy," Kay said, blinking back her own tears. "My Granny and my mother both got me started with them. I might just try that salad idea if you wouldn't mind."

"Of course I wouldn't mind. He told me how to make the dressing the very first time I asked, and I'd be proud to pass it along to you." She sighed and shook her head, sending tiny bits of green fire shooting all across the Formica table from her earrings and necklace. "He never did tell me what he soaked those apples in. I really wish he had now. That had to be what made them taste so good, since he used apples from wherever he could get them. He always promised to, but I know it's too late now."

Kay made real sure her face didn't reflect the odd little thrill that went through her belly at those words despite how sad she felt for Venus. That was one of the many ways she was so well matched with Adam.

Besides each other, they both loved a challenge more than pretty much anything else.

"It's a whole different thing," she said, "but will you let me send along a couple of slices of strawberry-rhubarb pie for you and Charlie? As a treat from me and Adam? Might be just what you both need after such a hard time."

Venus pursed her lips, but Kay could tell she was trying not to smile instead of fighting back a frown.

"Charlie does love strawberries. That would be just fine, and I sure do thank you."

Kay stood, trying to keep her mind from ranging too far ahead into how many dried apples she had on hand and how soon she could start them soaking.

"If you feel up to it tomorrow, I hope you can bring him by," she said. "We'd like to pay our respects and all. And be sure to let me know if there's anything else at all we can do."

Venus reached up and gave Kay's hand a quick squeeze.

"I sure will. To tell you the truth, I think that would cheer both of us up more than you know.

Right now I believe I'm going to finish up your good soup beans and the perfect coffee Adam so kindly made for me. And I'll write out that dressing recipe before I go."

Kay walked toward the kitchen, flashing Adam a thumbs up where Venus couldn't see. He blew her a kiss in return.

She did feel good about making her friend feel better, like she always did.

But she had her sights set on doing a good bit more than that if she could.

Chapter 2

SURE ENOUGH, Venus walked into the café at the very same time the next afternoon, with her own handsome husband by her side.

And since all four of them had been friends for well over half their lives, Kay couldn't imagine Venus with anyone else.

Charlie was as tall and lanky as Adam was medium-sized and sturdy. He managed to not be overshadowed by his wife's outfits, too, which endlessly impressed Kay. Today his shirt, pants, shoes, belt, and even his watch were a sharp charcoal gray, while she shimmered in a deep purple dress that went all the way down to her ankles.

Even in a remote little mountain town like Lightning Gap, the two of them somehow didn't seem to be showing off or putting on airs. They were simply being their comfortable, ordinary selves, and that's how they fit right in.

Of course living there her whole life and talking to people pretty much every day of it, Kay understood how *un*-ordinary the town and everyone there were better than most.

"I can't thank you enough for that pie," Charlie said after he held Venus's chair for her, rubbing his flat belly. "It's funny how a thing like that can lift up your spirits."

Kay gave him a quick hug before he sat.

"Well, it was the least I could do to help, and I'm glad it did. Me and Adam are real sorry about your father."

Charlie nodded and reached out for Venus's hand.

"I appreciate that. I'll miss him for sure." He smiled then, like the sun peeking through on a cloudy day. "Venus tells me your comfort food is exactly what I need."

Kay knew the flush in her cheeks showed just how pleased she was by the compliment, but she didn't much care. Her parents made sure to teach her not to be embarrassed to be good at something she loved.

"I'll do my very best for you, Charlie. How's chicken and dumplings sound? And I even tried my hand at your daddy's salad Venus told me about yesterday if you wouldn't mind to see how I did with it. People are telling me it's good, but I know you're the real experts."

This time both Charlie and Venus smiled for real.

"That sounds just right to me," he said. "He loved to cook for us almost as much as you do. I'm sure you did Daddy proud, but I promise to give you my honest opinion."

Kay didn't miss Venus's wink right before she turned away.

She was on the right track for sure.

But the real test would come once her friends got a bite.

She waited as long as she could stand before she checked back in with them, which meant until it was time for the steaming hot chicken and dumplings. Kay insisted on taking them herself, of course, even if one of the high school kids working the kitchen followed along to pick up the salad plates.

The entirely *empty* salad plates, she was pleased to notice.

"And how was everything?" she said, crossing her fingers inside her mind so she wouldn't drop the tray.

Both Venus and Charlie nodded, but Kay knew she'd missed the mark on her first try. Their smiles had an obvious dollop of *thank-you-for-trying-but...*

"That was just delicious," Charlie said, sitting back as his plates got swapped out. "The dressing was exactly right."

"And the apples?" Kay said, looking at Venus this time.

"They were real good, especially with the walnuts and all."

Kay raised one eyebrow and waited, a sure-fire habit she'd picked up from her own father.

"Well, you know," Venus said, glancing at Charlie. "That kind of thing is so hard to figure out, hon. Especially since you never got to try the ones Charlie's father made. Yours are so *good*, though. Did you use different apples, or soak them in different stuff?"

Kay's initial disappointment at not getting it right got chased away with the pleasure of being appreciated for her effort.

"All the same kind of apples, from an orchard out in Boun County. But you're right, I soaked them four different ways. I might have tried a couple more if you end up having room for dessert."

Charlie laughed as he picked up his spoon.

"I intend to eat every bite of this first, if that's what you're asking. Smells too good to let it go to waste. But if I ever don't have room for your dessert, that's how you'll know something's gone wrong with me."

Kay walked back over to the soda fountain, where Adam waiting with his own eyebrows raised.

"Not quite right," she said. "I felt sure the ones soaked in cider and cinnamon would be right."

Adam stepped out from his domain long enough to give her a one-armed hug.

"That's what that person over in Estonoa suggested, right? The cook at the Railsong Café?"

"That's right. He asked around for other ideas too, from the old folks who usually know all these kinds of secrets. I'll just have to hope I did better with the apple crisp and the hand pies."

She stopped for a second, trying to decide if she wanted to admit what she was thinking, and feeling.

As usual when it came to talking to Adam, the choice was an easy one.

"It's just that I feel so bad for folks when a thing like this happens. They lose someone they love, and one of the ways that person made them *feel* loved all at the same time. I figure if I can bring that one thing back, it's like making sure they get a hug when they need it, so they won't feel so sad and lonesome."

"That's what you do here every day, sugar pie,"

Adam said. "I'm sure you'll work it out for them, too."

But when Venus and Charlie ordered one each of the apple crisp and the hand pie—exchanging bites with each other halfway through—they had the same not-quite-there expressions.

"I really do think your pie crust is better than any I've tasted before," Charlie said, and Venus chimed in with the same about the apple crisp topping.

They each hugged her tight before they left, with a promise to stop back in the next day. Venus pulled Kay aside before they headed out into the early springtime evening.

"It means the world to him, you know, making all this effort for him. This is the most I've seen him smile since his daddy took sick. Don't worry yourself about getting things exactly right. What's that they say, it's the thought that counts?"

"It sure is. You all get some rest, and I'll see you tomorrow."

Kay let out a long sigh, but her mind was already sorting through what she could try next.

The café was still calm right before the big dinner rush they always had with chicken and dumplings, when they'd all work extra-hard for a bunch of extra-happy diners.

The only table without someone already tending to it was actually a booth against the wall painted deep pink. A tiny woman smiled at Kay, looking like a little girl against the booth's high back. Her brown hair sparkled with silver, but her face seemed oddly young for what had to be her late fifties. Or was it her sixties? Or maybe older than that, since it seemed like she and her husband had been part of Lightning Gap forever.

This was one of the rare times Kay never could tell for sure.

Carabelle Seagon, one of the owners of the Odds and Endings bookstore right across the street. That Victorian was painted a striking purple, and a fantastic rounded turret room at the very top of three stories made it stand out from all the rest.

The writers-in-residence who often stayed at Odds and Endings were some of Kay's favorite customers.

And the bookstore itself was pure magic.

"How are you today, Carabelle? Anything I can get for you?"

Carabelle nodded, her bright eyes sparkling as they usually were. As she and her husband Arthur often did, together or alone, she'd tucked herself into the booth with a book and a cup of tea for a little bit of quiet time.

"You can get yourself over here and sit down and talk for a minute," she said. "And tell me if I'm guessing right from my utterly shameless listening in on you and Venus and Charlie just now."

Kay let out a big belly laugh and walked on over, knowing she could never resist such a bold invitation.

"Now I can't wait to hear what you have to say."

Before Kay could look around to ask one of the great kids to bring her a cup of tea to match, one of the young men showed up with a cup, a saucer, and an adorable curvy teakettle full of hot water. A hand-made wooden box from a shop in town and full of tea bags already waited on the table beside Carabelle.

He grinned and took off before Kay could even say thank you.

"Since you're all set there," Carabelle said, "and I know you'll have a big rush in a little while with that dinner I can smell coking right now, I'll just jump right in. Sounded to me like you're trying to find the secret to someone's favorite apple pie."

Kay waited long enough to pour steaming hot water over a little bag of peppermint tea before she answered.

"That's awfully close, not that you're ever that far off. I was aiming for the filing Charlie's father made out of rehydrated apples and put in all kinds of things. I'm sorry to say he passed away without letting anyone know just how he did it."

Carabelle nodded as she finished what looked like raspberry tea, then plucked a bag of Earl Gray out of the box.

"I'm sure you know that's a hard thing to get right, even if you know each and every one of the secret ingredients. And I'll bet you know exactly *why* it's so hard, since you do such a wonderful job of doing it every single day right here."

Kay pushed her tea bag down into the water with the back of her spoon, watching it float up before she pushed it back down.

"Why yeah, I have a pretty good idea. There's something in the *way* they do it, the one who loves you that much. I don't mean the way they knead bread or that they stir everything exactly seven times or anything like that. I mean they have...a special touch."

"A touch filled with that love," Carabelle said. The citrusy bergamot aroma from her cup joined the peppermint already in the air. "And that's what you want to give back to them if you can."

Kay managed to nod, but now she stared at her cup through the faint blur of tears.

"That's just what I want to do, what I've *always* wanted to do. I know I can't ever bring that person back, and I wouldn't because that's just not the right way of things. But I get so attached to folks who come in here, and my friends even more so. I hate so much to see them hurting. Does that make sense to you?"

When Carabelle looked up and Kay blinked back her tears, Kay knew she'd found the right words. And said them to the right person.

"That makes all the sense in the world to me. That's part of the reason Arthur and I wanted to start a bookstore, and why we love it so. People might not get the same kind of comfort from a book as they do from someone taking care of them. At least the lucky ones who feel cared for. But for them and the ones who aren't so lucky, they can get so much from a book. From a *story*."

"You mean like a story they read when they were little? Or had read to them?"

Carabelle shrugged and smiled again.

"Sometimes that's it. We have people coming in all the time wanting to have the same version with the same cover and all of a book they loved when they were five years old. The thing is we get people looking for a book they've never read before too, and they light up when they see it. I know deep down that they'll get every bit as attached to that book as to one they read decades ago."

Kay held her teabag up by the string, letting it drain and spin over the cup.

"That's the best way I've ever head it said. About why Odds and Endings is so special, I mean. I wish I could work out how to do that same thing here. Especially for Venus and Charlie."

When she looked up, Carabelle surprised her with a wink.

"How about I send Arthur over here with a special book for you? One I know will turn into your favorite, and help you give folks that comfort you want to so badly?"

"How can you pick out a book like that for me?" Kay said, then shook her head. "I'm sorry, I don't mean to sound so rude and doubtful. I know Odds and Endings has done that very thing for me since I was a kid. But can it work if I don't even walk through the door?"

"You leave that to me, and to Odds and Endings. I'll make sure to send it over before you get too busy. That and a special ingredient all my own that I think will make all the difference."

Kay tried to find doubt or a joke or some kind of teasing in Carabelle's bright eyes, and she couldn't find a trace. Only the twin to her own desire, her own need, to help people who needed it.

"Thank you, Carabelle. I'll be looking for that book, and that secret ingredient, too."

Chapter 3

THE DINNER RUSH started earlier than usual, since a whole lot of people apparently needed their chicken and dumplings fix.

By the time Kay finally had a chance to sit down at Adam's soda fountain bar and catch her breath, a little brown paper bag with her name in Carabelle's loopy handwriting was already waiting for her.

She hadn't even seen Mr. Seagon or anyone else bring it in.

Inside waited what looked like an ordinary cookbook, with a brown fabric cover and the words "Feeding Family" in black lettering on the cover.

But when she looked closer, she realized the book was carefully hand made instead of coming from any kind of factory. She could see tiny, neat stiches along the binding, and the pages had a pleasing sort of uneven finish on the opposite side.

The only publisher mark she could find inside or out was the same stylized script "O & E" that she'd seen all over the bookstore.

She frowned at the table of contents, wondering if it had been water damaged at some point. All the other pages in the book had sharp, crisp print, in black ink that stood out against the thick, cream-colored background.

But the table of contents looked blurry. Unfinished.

As if it was only a stand-in before the final edition, maybe.

Kay jumped when Adam touched her shoulder. She looked around and realized only the usual after-dinner handful were still in the café.

"I'm sorry, I didn't mean to startle you," he said, sitting on the barstool beside hers. "I've been wondering what was in there all evening."

"It's okay, sweet pea. I just now got a chance to look. I think there's something else in the bag. Did you happen to see who brought it over? I got so busy I didn't see anyone."

He picked up the paper bag and reached inside.

"I didn't see either. I turned around and the bag was sitting right there in your usual spot. Huh, look at this."

He held up a thick, old-fashioned brown bottle about as long as his hand, stoppered with a bit of cork. And a single sheet of folded over paper.

"I'll let you read the note," he said. "While I do my best not to get into this until we know what it is. I'm sure the Seagons wouldn't give us anything bad, but I hate to waste something that was meant for you."

Kay handed the book to him and took the paper in return. More of Carabelle's handwriting waited inside.

My dearest Kay,

As it always does, Odds and Endings worked its magic.

This is your book.

I believe you'll find everything in these pages to give those who pass through your door what they need.

I'm not in the habit of giving away too many of my secrets, but I will tell you this.

When I need to find a special book, for myself or for someone else, I add one drop of the water in this bottle to my tea. Or my bourbon, depending on the time of day and what I'm looking for.

Then the magic of Lightning Gap and Odds and Endings shows me the way, so I can pass along what someone else needs.

I expect it will do the same for you.

If you need more, a woman who lives up on the ridge catches it from the rain during Lightning Gap's spectacular storms. She learned it from her mother and grandmother before her, so you can trust what she says.

I believe the two of you went to school together, same as Venus. Her name is Ivy Gweddon.

With love,

Carabelle Seagon

When Kay looked up, Adam had two small glasses and a bunch of his usual ingredients lined up on the counter. He'd added a few small brown bottles of his own, full of the herbal concoctions he was forever tinkering with. The whole box full of tools was there too, little scraping knives and eyedroppers and spoons and all.

The cookbook waited open beside him.

"What did you find in there?" she said.

"Well, I'm not sure yet, but it looks for all the

world like the tonic my papaw used to make when one of us was feeling puny. I saw what he put in, but I've never been able to get it just right. What was in the letter?"

"I'll let you read it in a minute. After we try your tonic."

She waited while he measured and mixed, ending up with a barely thickened beverage that was ever so slightly green. They each took a sip at the same time.

The drink exploded with bright citrus, smooth sweetness, and a lovely earth undertone she couldn't quite recognize. Perfectly balanced and altogether wonderful.

But Kay knew it wasn't quite right before Adam said a word.

He had that disappointed look in his eyes.

"That's about the closest I've ever gotten," he said. "It might be one of those things I'll just have to remember."

"Hang on, let me try something."

Kay pulled the cork out and picked up one of Adam's clean eyedroppers from his herbal kit. She added one drop of clear rainwater to each of their glasses. Adam swirled his, but he still looked doubtful.

"Just try it," she said, looking up from under her eyebrows with an I Dare You.

When he did, his eyes lit up and he grinned like a little boy.

"Wow, that made *all* the difference! I haven't tasted that since I was a goofy kid back in school. What's in that bottle?"

Kay wasn't at all surprised that her tonic tasted just the same. But she did feel a heck of a lot better.

"It's rainwater from up on the ridge," she said. "Let me see that recipe first, then I'll let you read Carabelle's letter."

Adam accidently flipped the book closed on the way over.

"I *am* a kid back in school. Klutzy as anything. It was on page..."

He scowled, but Kay pulled the book over before he could check.

She couldn't stop her grin when she looked back at the table of contents. The print was still a tiny bit blurry, but she could read the Desserts section toward the end just fine.

Complete with a heading called "Cooking with Dried Apples."

"Carabelle was right," she whispered. "The book is the door, and the rainwater opens it."

"What are you whispering about?" Adam said with a laugh. "Let me see."

Kay giggled and pulled the book away, holding it to her chest.

"I'll let you read it, but I've got to get something started for tomorrow. I'll need this." She popped the cork back in the brown bottle. "Don't worry, there's more where this came from. I think I know how to put the hug into my food now."

Chapter 4

THE NEXT AFTERNOON, Kay was ready and waiting when Venus and Charlie walked in.

They were both dressed down by their own standards, with her in black pants and a shimmering green jacket that fell in a dramatic sweep in the front and back. He wore plain old blue jeans, but his indigo blue button-up shirt fit without the usual cuffs or collar.

Kay met them at the door and linked her arms through one of each of theirs.

"I'm so glad you two could make it today. You've got me and Adam both trying all kinds of new things that we hope you'll like."

She walked them to their favorite table and watched Adam himself carry over two plates he'd been keeping on ice behind the soda fountain bar.

"Good to see you two," he said. "I'm real sorry about your father, Charlie. That's a rotten thing."

Charlie nodded, but he seemed distracted by the plate in front of him. Nothing more than a clever little arrangement of apples, sliced cheddar cheese, and a sprinkle of peppery greens, all on top of a crispy round cracker.

Pretty fancy for Kay's Café for sure, but not all that unusual.

The only strange thing was the faint reddish tint of the apples, and their vibrant cinnamon smell.

"Thank you for that, Adam," Charlie finally said. "He'd been sick for a while, but it's never easy."

"I hope cornmeal crusted trout will suit you both," Kay said, trying her best not to smile at the way Charlie kept glancing back at the apples. "That and a big mess of onions and peppers and potatoes."

Venus watched Charlie for a second before she picked up her little apple and cheese bite.

"That sounds fine to me, Kay. Sounds wonderful. Did you do something different with these today? They sure do smell good."

"I tried something new is all. Can't wait to see what you two think of it."

Charlie picked his up, then looked at Venus and smiled. They both popped the appetizers into their mouths at the same time.

And both opened their eyes wide only a few chews and a swallow later.

"That's *it*," Charlie said, staring at Kay. "That's exactly the same way Daddy made his apples. How did you do that?"

Venus only nodded and smiled, her eyes bright with what Kay knew had to be happy tears.

She let her grin break through at last, and saw Adam do the same.

"I soaked them in cider from over in Wolf Branch

with a little bit of cinnamon added in. I'm about as tickled as I can be that you like them."

Venus laughed and grabbed Charlie's hand.

"Like them? I know this won't make a lick of sense, but they taste like getting a hug from Charlie's father all over again." She reached out and took Kay's hand as well. "Thank you, hon. You have no idea what this means to us."

Kay covered Venus's hand with her own.

"Well, I do know it means the world to me to hear you say that. Once things settle down for you, come back by and I'll show you how I did it. Sound good?"

Venus squeezed her hands and let go, then pulled Charlie into a quick hug. He was beaming with his smile like the sun peeking out from a storm cloud.

"Sounds perfect."

Kay gathered up the empty plates and headed back to the kitchen, her full skirt swishing around her knees. Adam was working on a milkshake, but he caught her eye and blew her a kiss.

She knew she could never bring someone back once they'd gone on, and she still wouldn't want to.

But Kay couldn't wait to bring back those hugs every chance she got.

ABOUT KARI

The daughter, granddaughter, and great-granddaughter of coal miners, Kari Kilgore's wanderlust and imagination lead her all over the world on grand adventures. Her heart and family bring her home to her native Appalachian Mountains of Virginia. From that solid base, she and her husband Jason A. Adams bring those adventures to life in fiction.

Kari writes fantasy, science fiction, romance, mystery, and contemporary fiction, and she's happiest when she surprises herself. She lives at the end of a long dirt road in the middle of the woods with Jason, various house critters, and wildlife they're better off not knowing more about.

The Confidential Adventure Club

For Kari's exclusive free After The End stories and deleted scenes, discounts, early pre-sale releases, adorable pet photos, and a whole lot more not available anywhere else, swing by

www.ConfidentialAdventureClub.com.

Hope to see you there!

www.KariKilgore.com
www.SpiralPublishing.net

ALSO BY KARI KILGORE

I hope you enjoyed reading the stories in *Stepping Out of Reality* as much as I enjoyed writing them.

For more stories from the fabulous little town of Lightning Gap from *A Taste Just Like a Hug*, where Kay's Café and the wonderful food often make an appearance, visit www.KariKilgore.com/LightningGap.

If you'd like to catch up with Mark from *The Perfect Shade of Haint Blue* when he's all grown up, don't miss www.KariKilgore.com/VoicesThroughTime.

For more adventures from the Appalachian Mountains of Virginia and around the region, including Bountyfield, Estonoa, Lightning Gap, and more, head over to www.KariKilgore.com/TalesFromAppalachia.

If you're looking for more fantasy tales of all kinds, check out www.KariKilgore.com/Fantasy.

Be the first to know about release dates and check out more of my fiction, including almost every genre, at www.KariKilgore.com.

The Confidential Adventure Club

Want more fiction from Kari, including stories, discounts, and box sets not available anywhere else? Want to hear about locations, research, and other cool things that inspired these stories and beyond? Want all that and adorable pet photos, too?

Join The Confidential Adventure Club and get a thank you gift of a free short story and a whole lot more. www.ConfidentialAdventureClub.com.

Hope to see you there!

The Storms of Future Past Series:

Dreaming the Storm

Joining the Storm

Into the Storm

Fighting the Storm

Sensing the Storm: A Storms of Future Past Prequel

Storms of the Heart: A Storms of Future Past Romance

Storms of Future Past Books One through Four Collection

The Odd Society:

Independent by Means of Magic

Protected by Means of Magic

The Voices through Time Series:

Songs in the Mountain

Secrets in the Land

Walking the Ghosts: A Voices through Time Novella

Dispatches from the Galaxy Stories:

Restricted Species

The Becalmed

The Garbage Belt

Plurapod Pathogen

The Changes Cascade

Novels:

Until Death

The Dream Thief

Hand Me Downs

Protecting Her Own

Novellas:

Legacy of the Land

In the Pines

DNA Never Lies

The Box of Possibilities

Collections:

Fantastic Women: A Dark Fantasy Novella Trio

Fantastic Shorts: Volume 1

Near Future Forward (with Jason A. Adams)

Fantastic Shorts: Volume 2

Partners in Romance (with Jason A. Adams)

Dispatches from the Galaxy: A Space Opera Novella Trio

Fantastic Shorts: Volume 3

Escape into Romance: A Collection of Sweet Beginnings